PRAISE FOR *ORDINARY MATTER*

'Elegant, wise and humming with insight – this sublime collection proves that Elvery is in a class of her own.' **Toni Jordan**

'There is nothing ordinary about these stories – extraordinary, yes. Elvery takes inspiration from the few women scientists who have won Nobel Prizes, but then has the creative courage to follow those threads of inspiration wherever they may lead – often to very unexpected places. These stories gently and beautifully track the outward ripples of these women's scientific achievements, through the years and across decades. An experimental and literary triumph.' **Ceridwen Dovey**

'A beautifully crafted and moving collection of stories about women who change history while struggling against its constraints.' **Abigail Ulman**

'Daring, wholehearted and wickedly funny, each story in Elvery's *Ordinary Matter* expertly reveals an entire world – of love, hurt, healing; of ambition, discovery, and revenge. An utterly luminous collection from one of the country's most original voices.' **Brooke Davis**

PRAISE FOR *TRICK OF THE LIGHT*

'A complex emotional intimacy is present in all of Elvery's stories, but it's her inventive characters meeting original circumstances that makes *Trick of the Light* that rare thing: a page-turning short fiction collection.' **The Saturday Paper**

'Radiant, accomplished and exquisitely written, this is an outstanding collection.' **Ryan O'Neill**

'Elvery has a talent for portraying the minutiae of characters' lives and then suddenly stripping the banal away, so that we are left staring at the bare bones of a life … Elvery's debut reads like a triumph of excavation − a collection in which dark matter is exposed and subsequently transformed … An intriguing and powerful new writer.' **Overland**

'Elvery has a particular knack for getting into the heads of children and teenagers; her young characters are a compelling mix of naivety and recklessness, trusting of adults but constantly let down by them. Her adult characters are adrift but doing their best and remain hopeful to the end. Meticulously crafted … these are stories of subtle beauty and power.' **Books + Publishing**

'Laura Elvery's debut *Trick of the Light* introduces a genuine new talent to Australian literature. Her 24 stories contain vignettes as varied, poignant, funny and daring as anything I've encountered in years.' **Geordie Williamson**

Laura Elvery is a writer from Brisbane. She has a PhD in Creative Writing and Literary Studies. Her work has been published in *Overland*, *Griffith Review*, *Meanjin*, *Kill Your Darlings* and *The Big Issue* fiction edition. She has won the Josephine Ulrick Prize for Literature, the Margaret River Short Story Competition, the Neilma Sidney Short Story Prize and the Fair Australia Prize for Fiction. In 2018 Laura's first collection of short stories, *Trick of the Light*, was a finalist in the Queensland Literary Awards.

Book club notes are available at www.uqp.com.au

Also by Laura Elvery

Trick of the Light

ORDINARY MATTER

LAURA ELVERY

UQP

First published 2020 by University of Queensland Press
PO Box 6042, St Lucia, Queensland 4067 Australia
Reprinted 2022

University of Queensland Press (UQP) acknowledges the Traditional Owners and their
custodianship of the lands on which UQP operates. We pay our respects to their Ancestors
and their descendants, who continue cultural and spiritual connections to Country.
We recognise their valuable contributions to Australian and global society.

uqp.com.au
reception@uqp.com.au

Cover design by Josh Durham, Design by Committee
Author photograph by Trenton Porter
Typeset in 12/17 pt Bembo Std by Post Pre-press Group, Brisbane
Printed in Australia by McPherson's Printing Group

 Queensland Government   The University of Queensland Press is supported by the Queensland
Government through Arts Queensland.

 Australian Government   Australia Council for the Arts   The University of Queensland Press has been assisted
by the Australian Government through the Australia
Council, its arts funding and advisory body.

This project was supported by the Queensland Government through Arts Queensland,
the Queensland Library Foundation and Queensland Writers Centre.

A catalogue record for this book is available from the National Library of Australia.

ISBN 978 0 7022 6276 0 (pbk)
ISBN 978 0 7022 6398 9 (epdf)
ISBN 978 0 7022 6399 6 (epub)
ISBN 978 0 7022 6400 9 (kindle)

University of Queensland Press uses papers that are natural, renewable and recyclable products
made from wood grown in well-managed forests and other controlled sources. The logging and
manufacturing processes conform to the environmental regulations of the country of origin.

MIX
Paper from
responsible sources
FSC FSC® C001695

For my daughter, Harriet

CONTENTS

But the formative faculty of Earth does not take to her heart only one shape; she knows and is practised in the whole of geometry.

Johannes Kepler, 1611

YOU RUN TOWARDS LOVE

1903 | MARIE CURIE | PHYSICS

Prize motivation: 'in recognition of the extraordinary services they have rendered by their joint researches on the radiation phenomena discovered by Professor Henri Becquerel'

THE TRAIN MOVED FROM STATION to station through the French countryside. The windows showed flashes of buildings that were chalky, honey-coloured and soft. Faye turned her face towards the broiling world outside. Dusk was her favourite time of day. Further along the train carriage, she had spotted a man who used to be her lover.

Staying still in her seat, she tried to piece together the coincidence – on today of all days, on this, the same train to Paris. Coincidences kept her going; they fed her. Like the coincidence, two months ago, of seeing a photo in *Le Figaro* of this former lover beside a podium, flanking the Minister.

Finally, she came unsteadily up the aisle. She tapped Leon on the shoulder. 'Do you think it's fair that the Minister is on holidays in the snow while the country burns?'

~

Time seemed to telescope. Leon tried to gather his thoughts in time with the *chk chk chk* of the train's steel wheels on the track. One beat wouldn't do. A few beats, then. Before she arrived, he'd

3

had his head back on the seat, his eyelids at half-mast. He'd been thinking about wheat in the fields, a hare frozen beside the tracks, a red coupé appearing to rise briefly in the distance before vanishing behind the scorching wood on the hill. Seeing Faye tipping in the aisle, waiting for him to speak, he felt like the hare. He felt like a man twice his age, when he'd actually been half his age when they last saw each other. He'd always been curious about mathematics; till this point it had formed part of his rather ordinary and uninspiring career.

'Would you,' he finally replied, 'prefer the Minister holidayed in the desert?'

'It's not a good look, you can see that, yes?' She stood wedged between him and the seat in front, which was empty. She was rocking slightly and she hooked her left arm around the headrest and hugged her body into it. 'Your boss should work on his optics.'

~

Faye was certain he didn't have a woman in his life. He appeared scruffy and unencumbered. Tired-looking and twenty pounds skinnier than she remembered. Less muscle. His t-shirt with its print of the Hawaiian Islands, squashed and off-centre, had a small rip at the neck. She was prepared for him to see how she had aged. She was plumper, and her skin was no longer smooth and beach-freckled. Perhaps she would seem even shorter than before. Her posture had always been terrible. She presented her body in the aisle. He might or might not remember undressing her on a pebbled beach beside the Adriatic Sea. She had nothing to hide.

Leon cocked his head and widened his eyes. 'Ah, I think the Minister could not save us, even if he were here.' Playful again, as though she were a child.

'The reactors are struggling yet the Minister has given them permission to release hotter water into the rivers. Have you heard about the fish?' she asked.

'The fish?' he replied. 'The ones that will suffocate in hot water?'

She clapped her hands. 'One degree is all it takes. The margins are so fine. And then – *poof!* – they suffocate.'

'Imagine their shock. Those fish,' Leon said. 'In their very own home.'

The train undulated through the early night. Faye sat across from Leon. Dark blue and grey fabric upholstered the seats, embroidered with stars as big as hands. Cigarette smoke drifted from another passenger. The smell of a woman's herbaceous perfume. Most of the seats in the car were empty. But before she sat, Faye saw a woman half her age, a young mother sitting with a boy, sharing a paper sack of sweets between them.

'Where are you going?' Leon asked.

'Paris.'

'Ha. You chose the right train.'

'You?'

'Paris,' he said. A faint line in the sand.

So they would not tell each other anything, then. Fine, she thought.

'I'm meeting someone there,' he added.

'Will she be waiting for you?'

'No. I'll make my own way.'

'Do you have a gift for her?'

'It isn't that sort of meeting.'

But Faye barrelled on. 'When we hop off, we could buy her a

bunch of flowers. What is her favourite colour? Or perhaps a fan? A cold bottle of beer and some boots filled with snow?'

'You bought me some terrific gifts, didn't you, way back? You mustn't think I've forgotten them.'

'Oh, I've tallied them up, in fact, and worked out how much you owe. Interest, too. It'll be a great windfall when we hop off this train and you take me to a cash machine.' She rubbed the tips of her fingers together, gleefully, close to his face.

He laughed. He folded his arms.

'This woman – I hope you brought something better to wear,' she said.

'This is my favourite.' He ran his hands down the front of the hideous t-shirt. Had she hurt him, or was he playing? 'What about you – why the trip to Paris? Returning? One way?' This turn in conversation suddenly felt tedious. It could have been anyone speaking these words about tickets and timetables. She sensed the conversation lull; it weighed heavy on her like fatigue.

She said, 'I want to shut down one of the reactors.'

He turned his face to her. 'Say that again.'

'A reactor. I plan to shut one down. Make it stop. Cease.' She pushed her fingers through her hair and checked for loose strands that she let flutter to the carpet.

He stared. 'Do you expect to knock on the door and see a giant stop button? Or a huge dial with a temperature gauge written in red numbers?'

She searched her mind for a wounding they might have inflicted on each other. A cruelty she may have meted out thirty years ago. She was proud of herself when she came up short, pleased that she'd exercised kindness in her past without knowing that it might pay off.

'And I'll just turn it?' Faye said, finally animated. 'Like this?' She remembered his teasing. She'd never missed it and now that she was older, it seemed even more childish. That he hadn't grown out of it was interesting. She didn't need his help at all. Perhaps her comment about the t-shirt had done it: he'd always been sensitive.

'Yes,' he said. 'Just like that.'

Faye laughed, covering her mouth. The coffee cart trundled down the aisle, and Faye shoved her legs out of the way. After it passed she stood and stretched to the ceiling, then down to her toes. She felt her spine unbuckling, recognised the ache in her once-unnoticeable joints. Her long blonde-grey hair swept across Leon's shoulder. Then he patted her arm and her skin buzzed, as if it had been kissed, which it had. That sum was easy: thirty years ago. They had last kissed in 1973. From the corner of her eye, Faye saw the mother with the little sack of sweets open her coat pocket once more, saw the child slide his hand into that dark, woollen space.

At last the train stopped. Leon had a big bag with him, which irritated her. Through the narrow carriage door they shuffled onto the platform with the dozen or so other rumpled passengers. Across the tiles and through the turnstiles, all the while with that damn bag bumping against his hip. White nylon with a red and black stripe on the side – a sports bag. They were already old; they shouldn't be adding bulk to their frames.

Faye grabbed Leon's hand but only for a few seconds. He glanced at her hand as it left his.

'This way,' she said. She trotted ahead to cross the dark street, and he slung the bag across his body and increased his pace to keep up, taking long strides in his grey sneakers.

The evening held the heat from the day like a bell jar. All the daily newspapers and the afternoon bulletins published stories about the heatwave, the sunburn, city waifs jumping about in fountains, the elderly unable to calibrate themselves and the nurses who worked through the night to try. It was the hottest summer for more than five decades.

On the kerb was a mound of garbage bags, one with a leering slashy smile of a rip. The ripe gorge of rotten apples and courgettes and aubergines turned in the air. A pair of brown dogs nosed at a cement trough beneath a drinking tap. Faye and Leon moved below apartments that hummed with air conditioners. Lights in the *pied-à-terres* were ablaze. Parisians were restless, unable to sleep.

They passed a shuttered phone shop. They passed a laundrette where a skinny teenager lounged on a white machine, seemingly stunned by the churn of the clothes and the extra heat being generated. They saw a narrow wine-coloured bar. People stood outside smoking and pressing handkerchiefs to their throats, wiping hands across their foreheads. A young woman with a glossy black bob plucked at her t-shirt for a billow of relief.

For a long time Faye had forgotten what it meant to protest, to be furious. Years passed in which she'd tried on naivety, like a garment, looking at it this way and that, waiting for it to reflect something good back to her. At times it worked. She'd tried to trick herself into not worrying about a potential nuclear accident or nuclear fallout or nuclear waste. But the chilling simplicity of the mathematics involved when it all came down to one degree more, two degrees more.

She thought he understood this. Thirty years ago they'd gathered to protest, and together they ran towards trouble, towards the thing she was sure they could prevent.

~

They stepped into a park. Leon thought it was too hot to hold hands, but he saw people old and young clutching each other, fanning themselves while they strolled along the avenue of trees. One man walking on bowed legs reminded Leon of his own father, who was getting knocked around this summer in his apartment in Nemours. He should telephone and check on him again. Remnants of picnics were scattered on the ground where young families lay in the emerald-green grass. Two men kicked a football beside a striped rug.

'They're having to harvest the grapes early,' Faye said. 'I read that too.'

~

They walked the length of the garden. She opened her mouth to talk about death again – humans this time, not fish – but closed it. When they were young, Leon had never known her to be this grim and so it was pride that kept her from showing she had not lightened in her old age but darkened. This heatwave – inching beside them all during the day and looming over them at night – felt catastrophic. Sweat stewed down her spine.

Then up ahead she saw a crowd. It took Faye less than a second to recognise their roiling anger, the twitch and hopefulness: it was a protest. Or, rather, when she looked closer, it had been, outside the headquarters at Rue La Fayette. The facade was imposing grey stone, with three tall doors heavily caged and the company logo, *Areva*, on two discreet plaques beside the central entrance. There was no way they were getting in – these ten or twenty people in shorts and sneakers and caps. Faye's body flushed just thinking of the heat they were generating, in such tight proximity. The whole place might incinerate. Fragments of glass glittered on the ground in bright, sharp piles. Faye pointed up to show Leon: the glass must have fallen from the awning, smashed in the protest. Three or four trolleys were on their sides, and a bin, and chairs and a table. Across the street two men and a woman with blue hair climbed in through a broken shop window and seconds later emerged carrying bottles of beer.

'The fish,' she whispered. 'The rivers will be filled with dead fish.'

~

Leon turned to Faye. He knew all this, of course. And he knew how such an image was unlikely to cause a stir in the minds of the French people, as hard as that was to believe. Who cared, really, about fish anymore? Who cared about one or two or even three degrees?

'Let's get a drink,' he said. 'We can find somewhere cool and talk properly.'

'What about your date?'

'I'll find a phone.' He fanned his hands in front of his face. How was it possible he felt even warmer than before?

Faye nodded, and he led the way to the kerb and into the street. He glanced left and swivelled slightly back. He went to speak to her. He heard his name. A shout.

'Leon!'

~

Faye ran to his side and so did a young woman in a pink dress who said she knew first aid. Faye's mind kept skittering about the place. Panicked voices and the noises of the city and the streetlights and the maddeningly hot air. It was impossible to focus on what was in front of her. Back in time: Leon's body beneath hers on a mattress somewhere in Montpellier, her fingers plucking at the fine hair on his chest, trying to find a spot where he could be tickled. Forward in time: the two of them at a bar ordering wine.

Hard to pin life down to the present moment where Leon lay on the scorching black bitumen. All because he had stepped a second too soon and had looked at Faye for a second too long and the white delivery van had arrived at this part of Paris at this precise moment and struck Leon on the side of his tall, wiry body, which suddenly appeared very fragile.

The girl in pink told him, 'We're going to move you onto your side.'

They did, then tilted his head back gently. The skin on his jaw was rough. He lay on his side, eyes closed, not moving, but breathing.

His unzipped bag had spilt its contents onto the road. Sheets of papers sheathed out around his body like leaves. Not a change of clothes. No romantic date, then, indeed. Faye saw what had been in his bag all along. Documents. Carefully worded briefs, set on government letterhead. Pages and pages with information about temperature peaks and troughs, about numbers of people dead. She lifted some sheets from a pile and scanned the top one.

12 August 2003. 273 casualties.

13 August 2003. 189 casualties.

'Emergency,' she said. She dropped the pages and stood, raising her voice up into a night sky that refused to cool. 'This is an emergency.'

GRAND CANYON

1911 | MARIE CURIE | CHEMISTRY

Prize motivation: 'in recognition of her services to the advancement of chemistry by the discovery of the elements radium and polonium, by the isolation of radium and the study of the nature and compounds of this remarkable element'

FRANK WAGNER, TWENTY-FOUR YEARS OLD, wearing a bow tie and tails, and with a face like a fish, needs to piss. His host, Mrs Andrew Carnegie, is not the person to ask for directions. The rules of the Curies' visit have been laid out for him in very clear terms. Frank is not permitted to sit with the family at the table, having been employed only to carry their bags, keep the louses and the slobberers away, make sure the fans do not scare the ladies onto a ship back to France and, soon, to drive them west. After the war, Frank caught the IRT subway to Flatbush to work at a factory that made babbitt metal bearings. And now here he is: a man with a key in his pocket that unlocks a room at the Waldorf–Astoria.

The famous and remarkable Madame Curie has two daughters. It being their first time here, they are naive in American ways. Irene is twenty-three. Frank has hefted her bag, offered gum, listened to her attempts to speak English. A little reserved, but in that pleasing way where she lets others speak first, and for longer. Though not an intellectual himself, Frank has picked Irene as the genius of the two.

And then there's Eve.

15

Just sixteen. Less terse than her mother, which is to be expected on account of her age. So confident! So lively! He is not a man impressed by fancy clothes, which is good, since Eve's clothes are too big for her. (Hand-me-downs from her sister? How much money do scientists make?) The whole get-up – the coat, the hat, the dark brown heels with the chalky scuffs along the side – is not quite how American girls dress, but it's only slightly off, like a bear with a mouse or a pie made of eggs. About the scuffs: perhaps at home in Paris, she is a hiker? An adventurer? More than once, Frank has dreamt of returning with her. To hold her purse under the Eiffel Tower, impressing her with his knowledge of many different cheeses. *It is custom*, she might say, *for a man to kiss a girl beneath the cherry blossom. Would that be – how you say – 'okay with you', an American man in Paris?* Yes, he would accept, if that is the custom.

Frank now raises a hand, and within seconds a servant comes round and directs him to the bathrooms. 'Wow,' he says, actually out loud, having never seen a bathroom like this. Luckily, the servant is gone – what sort of a man wants another man to hear him say *wow*? Frank licks a finger and drags it a short way down a wall that has a grand mirror at each end. The bathroom is shiny and high-ceilinged, like a church. He could pray in here, if he had to. If Mrs Carnegie burst in here demanding that he get on his knees and pray. Sure thing. He'll do whatever these ladies ask of him.

Especially Eve. Frank unbuttons his fly and muses over the three conversations he's managed with her thus far: that's one per day and not bad for trying.

First conversation.

Eve: Mr Wagner, what are these?

Frank: Please. Call me Frank. That's a chrysanthemum. You ain't never seen one before?

Eve: Perhaps.

(Here, the young girl shrugged and held her shoulders for a brief moment right up near her ears. Her shoulders were not bare but covered in a filmy, silky fabric – Frank doesn't know the names of things young ladies wear. Wow. That such a fabric could produce such an ache in him.)

Second conversation.

Frank: Hello.

Eve: Hello. Good morning.

Third conversation.

Eve: Oh. Mr Wagner.

Frank: Do you need—?

Eve: Thank you, no.

Frank: Well. Goodnight.

Eve: Goodnight.

He's at the toilet pissing, taking in the gleam of the Carnegies' white tiles. The first two conversations were fine. Light, airy, attractive words involving subject matter becoming of a young lady, like *flowers*. You could say it was perfect subject matter. Those French people and their flowers! His brother, Clyde, back home in Pines, Ohio, who didn't know shit about sticks had been right. For once in his life!

But conversation number three smells a bit rotten, actually – yes, it's like he's left a bag of fruit somewhere and, remembering it, his brain goes *oof!* He used to get in trouble for this at school. Brain wandering, brain wandering – thinking of cold slices of pear, thinking of a girl's fingers on his groin (brain hopeful), thinking of round buttocks on the hot sand of Coney Island (brain memory) – then the teacher is screeching at him and *oof!* Gotta control the brain wandering. A new goal, perhaps.

Still pissing now – something to be proud of? Duration of piss?

Who knows? Most likely long duration of piss due to Mrs Carnegie serving onion soup, watermelon salad, champagne, iced tea, hot tea. Lots of liquid, period. Most regular days, he has two cups of coffee, tops, and a mouthful of radon water before bed. Frank is thinking of an alternative scenario about conversation number three, working it hard like raw dough. Is it possible that by putting her foot in the door of her hotel room at the Waldorf–Astoria the girl did not mean to wedge it shut against him? Alternative: she was actually trying to keep it open? Is it possible that the language barrier or French lady manners made it difficult for Eve to express her sixteen-year-old fledgling desire for him, Frank, one-time owner of three baby bear cubs?

Pissing done, buttoning up fly. All right, yes, the knock on her hotel room door had been late. And the chrysanthemum he popped into his top pocket on the way out of his own hotel room was a hasty, potentially unusual, addition. But what if Eve or her sister required something? That's where his brain had gone to make him rise from his bed and pad down the hall. Maybe their bodies were stuck on continental time, and they would be awake and greet him warmly: Irene at his feet, easing off his shoes; and Eve near his head to touch him on the temples? Would he like a refreshment? At eleven o'clock at night? It is the French way, after all. Or perhaps they were hungry and didn't know how to ask, and they were stuck, sobbing about Americans' lack of hospitality. The girls spoke some English. Their French was incomprehensible to his ears, but the sound of it coming from Eve's lips was like a vast and perfect galaxy. It was a bowl of strawberries and cream. Her voice was a light on a darkened stage coming up on his shabby upbringing in Pines, Ohio. He could learn French one day.

The soap – what is that scent? Frank rubs his hands vigorously under the spout and sniffs the tips of his fingers. He suffers from a skin condition that, thankfully, hasn't flared up for two weeks. In the mirror, his cheeks are smooth and clear. He has a sudden but not unexplainable desire to masturbate, quickly, in the Carnegies' bathroom. It's the soap that does it. It's the soap and remembering those buttocks on Coney Island when he was fifteen years old and visiting his cousin with the limp in New York City for the first time.

Eve.

Her name itself is a low and fruitful moan, punctuated by a bite of the lips. *Vvvv.*

Before things become too risky, he heads out through the bathroom door and back to the dining room. Frank would like to compliment Mrs Carnegie on the plushness of her towels. Would that be all right to say? Would the brittle and intimidating but also extraordinary Madame Curie pushing her beef and white beans around the plate overhear this and be invigorated by thoughts of, *Oh, what an observant man!* Observation being vital to the conduct of a scientist. Surely a trait she would appreciate in a son-in-law. Mr Curie is fifteen years gone, and Mr Carnegie almost two years. Mrs Carnegie is a generous host. She is plain and very, very rich. If Frank got lost in this enormous house, stayed here for some time, he doubts she would catch him for ages.

The dinner table seats a dozen. The women are safe with these people, though he cannot remember their names – a professor of something from upstate New York, a railway man, an oil man, a man in dynamite. Flowers in crystal vases have been placed along the length of the table, and tall candlesticks too. The other men seem much more comfortable in their suits than Frank feels. Standing in a room off to the side, he peers round but is careful not to stare at Eve too much. Instead he spreads his attention among the old, the boring, the hard of hearing, the dim, the ugly, the uninspiring. Eve leans into her sister – a bit wonky-looking, pale, pinch-nosed – and they touch their spoons together. The spoons are like two silver tongues. Even the *ting!* sets his mind alight. The girls giggle and do the spoon thing again. Must be a sister thing. Or French thing? Mrs Carnegie has served Horton's ice cream in three different flavours. Eve darts a finger up, and this time Frank cannot look away. The cream from her bottom lip, it gets swept up into her small wet mouth. Those dark eyes and milky skin. The ice cream reminds Frank of the soap in the bathroom. He thinks of the girl's finger, her tongue. In a week, they will go to the Grand Canyon, together.

They're on the road, heading west. They stop in Greensboro, North Carolina; and Fayetteville, Arkansas; and Amarillo, Texas, where they get to a roadside kiosk and Eve asks Frank to buy her and her sister a Coca-Cola. He fishes two nickels from his pocket, thinking he'll be able to watch her take a sip. Instead, they slide the bottles into bags at their feet, saying they'll take them home. Do the French not have Coca-Cola? What else do these mysterious women go without?

There are seven of them in two automobiles: the three Curies, Professor Jansen from New York, Professor Harrington from Virginia, Mrs Meloney, the lady who organised this whole thing and brought the three women across the Atlantic, and Frank. They are driving at night, the cold desert air coming in through the windows and sending Frank's brain tumbling back to a night in his old neighbourhood in Pines when he and his brother were out stealing copper pipes to sell to Mr Adquist and they'd heard a shout, then beyond the fence they saw two men lifting a girl into the cold, dark mouth of the woods. Frank made eye contact with her, briefly, the whole lot, but wordlessly he and his brother decided to clang the pipes around, speaking over each other about the copper, about how they'd better hurry before whoever these people were came home. All so they could pretend the maybe-bad thing with the girl wasn't happening. Because who knows? Maybe it didn't happen. Maybe they got it wrong.

The next morning, the sky all splotched with colour like three flavours of Horton's ice cream, the girls announce they've never ridden a horse, and Harrington says he's heard about some Indian ponies on a reservation nearby. So they take a detour and communicate, quite easily, with the Indians about what they want them to do. The Indians stand the cranky creatures on a ridge high above the valley. Frank chugs on a warm Coca-Cola. The sun is doing damage to the follicles on his face. He has his sleeves rolled up, suspenders and a hat from Krugman's in Brooklyn. His cousin took him there in his first week in New York City. He can feel his cheeks broiling, and the backs of his hands, all of it searing.

The girls have mounted the horses. Eve is a pale lily. The girls are waving. 'Wave, everybody!' someone says. So they wave. Let's get this show on the road, Frank thinks. Madame is feeling unwell today and sits with Mrs Meloney, who pats her hand, in the back seat of the Packard Twin Six four-passenger Special Touring – a glorious automobile. Frank could cry sick and go and luxuriate in the back seat too under the soft top. The sun is hot. What are they trying to do? Ride to the Grand Canyon? What with the burning sun and the capillaries on his face – he inherited his ma's capillaries – Frank is not his usual gentlemanly self. Let them ride ponies. He is, as his ma likes to say, pooped. Why does he need to be out here watching it? Isn't there a nice cool well he can dunk his burning face into?

The girls' pelvises are rocking backwards and forwards out there past the wells and the little houses painted yellow. What did Frank expect? His first Indian reservation? Teepees perhaps, and feathers. Instead the Indian kids are running around like nothing exciting is going on at all – do they not care about French people? Or about how many tonnes of pitchblende the girls' mother sifted through to find smidgens of radium? It makes Frank think of the copper pipes he and Clyde stole to sell to Mr Adquist. In a similar vein to Madame's efforts, when you think about it. You take a material from deep underground, you move it around, or sift through it, or drive up to the Adquist place in Clyde's truck and honk and Mr Adquist comes out in his dressing-gown, holding a mug of beer for them to share before he sorts through the lengths of copper. That kind of thing.

The girl in the woods. Well, she'd probably been fine. The most likely scenario – off the top of his head – was that it had been Halloween, the screams being part of it. That she had known those boys carrying her away, two limbs each. Yes, that was it. Nothing bad whatsoever was happening out beyond the rows of dahlias and the bricks stacked ten high to stop the crows from getting to the chicken coop. For a while he wondered if the girl – well, it wasn't – but he wondered if it may have been Katherine O'Kelly. From science class, and from Sunday school. The week after the copper and the woods, sure, she seemed different at school. Clyde didn't know what the heck Frank was going on about and couldn't he drop it? When your older brother tells you to drop it, drop it you do. Like when your cousin with the limp takes you to a titty bar down a set of stairs on your first night in New York City and both of you are immediately booted out: you drop it. You do not raise that embarrassing scene again with your cousin, the one with the limp.

Finally: they arrive at the Canyon in the late afternoon. Streaks of gold and orange swim from the rock to the sky, sharing the colours between them. Out of the Packards everyone climbs, and they follow the signs to South Rim. A great brown eagle swoops from one speck of a perch of rock to another.

Frank is obliterated by the size of the Canyon, by its colour and depth. By the idea it had been formed by God, the same God who'd watched on that time Frank looked after three baby bear cubs till the smallest one fell into a trap and died. He is obliterated by Eve, her bravery, her proximity to the edge of the hole right now while he stands away from the edge, frozen. The hole is a mile deep. He is obliterated by the idea that those Indians might have legends about this place. What did all this mean to those kids whose ponies the girls borrowed and sat on and dug their heels into? The sky, most likely: the Indians likely had stories about the sky.

He realises all his life has been a series of obliterations.

He thinks of his ma's shabby house – the plinky piano wedged onto the back porch, empty soda cans in the garden beds, her vast collection of gravy boats – tucked into the bottom of the canyon like a stone in a shoe. Frank, obviously not always wishing his mother could hear his thoughts, wants her to know he is thinking of her. Here at South Rim, the rock is layered like splodges of buckwheat pancake batter. All these dead rocks, thrumming with life. This current job of his – bag-holding, keeping the public at arm's length from Madame Curie and her girls – that he should be so close to these women when he's a nobody who will leave no impression on the world after he's gone. Just another obliteration. Soon the three ladies will go back to Paris.

'Some place,' is what he says, lifting his eyes back to Eve, who has gone out further, without him noticing.

She seems to be staring into the void. Imagine being able to do such a thing, at any age.

'As long as I live,' she says simply.

It's enough, though, isn't it, thinks Frank. *As long as I live.* 'Miss Curie, please come away from the edge.'

Irene, who is crouched on a rock with her skirt gathered beneath her legs, glances up and over.

Frank sees the neat square heels of Eve's boots, delicate against the rocks. The scuffs that have always been there, well, they stand out even more in the golden hour. She is sort of swivelling on the heels of her boots, no longer on an Indian pony, waving from its warm back, or from a railing the length of a white cruise ship. He steps closer.

Madame stands some distance away with Mrs Meloney and the two professors. Mrs Meloney is pointing things out to Madame, who holds a hand against her forehead. Frank has barely dared to approach her this whole trip. He's carried her suitcases without making a sound. Madame has asked him mildly and politely for things, and once waved him over to help when she couldn't unclasp a tin of Altoids. When Mrs Meloney had to cancel engagements because Madame needed to see a doctor, Frank stayed close to her daughters. Mostly, their mother has remained a mystery. That such a woman exists. And such a mind. Frank is obliterated once more. Dressed darkly again, Madame is a spindly blackbird on the buttery ridge.

'Eve?' Frank says. 'You're too close there, Miss.'

She turns, and he catches the musicality of her face, the sharpness even in her eyes, which seem half-opened most of the time. The skin on his cheeks stings while he watches this beautiful creature raise a hand to her forehead. She is gazing at something behind him.

'Hey,' a voice comes from over his shoulder.

Frank turns, achingly, away from Eve.

Professor Harrington calls out, 'Wagner!'

Madame has fallen onto her side, her black dress trapped under her like a terrible wave. He catches sight of her white face. Her eyes are closed, her mouth is slack. What is going through her mind, so far from home?

Here is a life he can save. Swift like a coyote, Frank bounds, scrambles up the rock on all fours. He thinks he hears two pairs of small boots running after him.

SOMETHING CLOSE TO GOLD

1935 | IRÈNE JOLIOT-CURIE | CHEMISTRY

*Prize motivation: 'in recognition of their
synthesis of new radioactive elements'*

I SWEPT THE SAND FROM THE HALLWAY. We had tried, in the past, to vacuum it up. A strange thing about the Sunshine Coast that summer was the cyclone season from up north encroaching in new ways: coming further south, and earlier than usual. The beaches near us were wild, with signs from lifesavers closing them more often than they were open.

Up on tiptoes I reached for a bottle of cheap merlot. I gulped a few mouthfuls from a tumbler. I opened my laptop to the news, then clicked on a story about cyclones. A few clicks later, I was reading an article about a female orca whose baby had died within an hour of birth. For seventeen days, the mother pushed the baby along the west coast of the United States, nudging it and balancing it on her head. I took my laptop from the kitchen and headquartered myself in bed. I read the rest and wept. I saw the calf's snub beak and its throat, slightly peachy. I felt an ache, my heart stretched thin.

Frederic appeared in the doorway. He knew where to find me, upset but regal against the pillows. Another man might have tried to prise the laptop from me, but he reached for the covers and climbed into bed too. We searched for pictures of the killer whale mother together.

The next morning I interrupted him in the garden. He was watering the heavy grey pots lined up beside the shed. He nosed the spout of the watering can into the basil, into the tomatoes, the radishes. I'd told him they were silly things to buy, but he'd coaxed life from them.

'Frederic?'

'Yes, love?'

He didn't know what was coming, so he still held the green can. In his other hand was a clump of mulch. I knew he would remember these ghoulish props. I took a breath, glanced around at the mounds of mown grass, at what my husband was trying to do with our garden. I rarely came out here.

I said, 'You asked me to tell you when I couldn't do this anymore.'

He didn't move, except to nod. I could feel his heart from where I stood. I felt its twang and its throb. The skipping it was doing, the plummeting.

He made a joke: 'Yep. You tell me when it happens.'

'I mean that I can't do—'

He put the watering can on the grass and let the mulch drop. 'I know,' he said, turning to show me half his face. Pink flushed. A too-big smile. 'I know.'

I clipped the leash onto the dog's collar and moved the water bowl close to her face with the tip of my running shoe. Frederic waved from the front door as I took off for the beach two streets away, the dunes always bringing to mind a little village buried underneath. At school I'd played touch football. I was never going to be captain, but I liked to yell at everyone regardless. I was fast and good at geeing up my teammates. I often spoke this way to the dog, telling her she could do it, telling her to hustle. She was a white Maltese terrier whose puzzled face – I thought, anyway – suggested she often forgot who I was, had no idea how she'd ended up living in our house. I yelled because I loved her.

I didn't have a lot of friends. My workmates tried hard, but they disappointed me. I knew they met up on weekends without me. They insisted it was kiddie-park stuff, noisy playgrounds, barely time to chat at all. But I was no-one's first thought. Frederic loved me, adored me so much it was embarrassing. He thought I was bright and sharp and hard. I thought that my cynicism let his kindness come through more clearly. What could be more cynical than that?

Enough, I thought as we jogged towards the beach. *No more.* I felt as light as a biscuit. No more. All of it: a blooming belly underneath specially bought dresses, a crib, feathery muslin wraps, a car seat. A baby's bald head cradled in my palm. I felt it peeling away.

Days before, at our fertility clinic appointment, I'd listened to the doctor go on and on. I'd watched his mouth open and close, his hopeful face lean towards us, the framed certificates above his head, while on the other side of his desk I nodded, saying in my head, *Okay, all right, it isn't going to happen.* It was a release like a knife in me. I'd made up my mind. The universe didn't care if I could have children. It wouldn't care if I decided to stop trying. But maybe it could feel my relief at this; perhaps the universe lets up when we give up, and we slip through a zip in the fabric, the universe accepting us, finally, because we are demanding one less thing from it.

The melaleucas that lined the edge of the footpath were throwing themselves sideways. A searing, sandy wind had picked up and the whole place looked like it was swirling. The dog must have felt the wind in her mouth, and she barked as if to get it out. The beach was empty. The dog skittered, nose first, down the sand, and that's how I found the baby. She was on her back, mewling, where the sand met the water.

I scooped her up and held her tight against the wind. She was completely drenched. Trails of seaweed wound around her fat little legs that I pictured kicking furiously in the water – the baby was missing a sock. I laid her on the ground, her cries strengthening, as I took off my jumper to wrap her up. Not knowing what else to do, I headed for the path. The dog wagged her tail and snapped at the wind.

Then I saw it. Bolted to a tree beside the boardwalk was a sign – the size of a postcard, weathered timber, painted white – that I'd never noticed before. Its message:

Lost on the beach? Found on the beach? Call 1800 975 710.

I took a photo of it on my phone and ran home with the baby in my arms. The dog raced ahead, her leash snaking behind.

Hours later I sat on our bed. The phone was tight in my hand. I couldn't stop watching Frederic cuddle the baby. He bobbed up and down. The two of them were dangerously close already.

'Sweetheart?' he said. 'You'd better call them.'

It rang and rang. As I was about to hang up, a voice clicked in. 'Thank you for calling the Department of Reunification and Wilderness Finds.'

I had never heard of this department. But it was true I'd forgotten to vote in the previous state election, so there could very well be entire departments I'd never heard of.

'I found a baby, a girl, just now, a few hours ago, on the beach near my house. And I saw this number on a sign. She's so little.'

'Are you seeking to keep her?' the man asked.

I heard background office noises and the *tack tack* of a keyboard. 'Keep her?'

'Are you in a position to *keep* the baby?'

I stared at Frederic. He kept returning to the mirror in the hallway, his face seeming to reflect a disbelief in this good fortune.

'We are.'

'Then I will now take you through a series of questions designed to assess your eligibility to keep any babies you find in the wilderness.'

'This was a beach.'

'Is a beach not wilderness?'

Pure poetry. From a bureaucrat. I wondered if he ever wrote things in a notebook at night before turning out the light as I did. *This* was the man who would decide our fate.

'Well, I suppose,' I said. 'The beaches up our way are pretty wild.'

'That's fine,' the man said. 'Let's begin. First question: Do you have any children?'

How many people had asked me that?

'No,' I answered.

'Have you suffered fewer than or greater than five miscarriages?'

I knew that Frederic, if he could hear this, would baulk at the question, but something in the man's voice made me trust him.

'Greater than,' I whispered.

'Has your extended family mourned with you on three occasions or more? Or fewer than three occasions.'

'More than three,' I answered.

'Have you listened to their good wishes, their condolences, listened to them say words to the effect of *I do not know what to say*, collected their flowers off your front step, and told them almost everything about your body, including but not limited to its uterine lining?'

'Yes.'

'Do you strongly suspect that your trauma is making it hard for friends and family to parent their own children, paint the house, check for fresh vegetables in the crisper, choose which colour socks to wear?'

'I do. Absolutely.'

'Please hold.'

The clap and vapour, the bells and pipes of the department's hold music will always remind me of that tiny creature. Down the hall Frederic and the baby resembled a pendulum. They were rocking to their own rhythm. It was just me with the phone to my ear, and I hated the sound of my breath, alone, echoed back to me.

Then the line clicked back in. 'Ma'am?'

'Yes, here.'

The baby was closer to me now, Frederic having bobbed his way over to the edge of the bed where I lay on my side. The baby reached out and tried to take my cheek in her mouth. Her brown eyes shone and looked away to the left, like she was searching for predators. She had found my cheek and wanted it for herself.

'Yes?' I repeated. My whole being was a question mark curled up on the bed.

'I can confirm that you are eligible to keep the baby you found in the wilderness.'

'Oh my god.'

'Please name the baby – nothing ridiculous, but that's my

personal opinion, not the position of the department – and register yourselves as the baby's new legal guardians within thirty days using the paperwork I'll send you shortly.' He paused. 'Keep her safe.'

'Yes, sir.'

'Congratulations,' he said, clearing his throat. 'All clear?'

My heart doubled. 'Thank you, yes.'

The line clicked out and the man was gone.

Without saying a word, we took the baby into the spare room that we'd never filled with much and laid her on the bed. Her arms and legs arced gently as if she was making an angel in the snow. We gazed down upon her.

Everything looked different now that we were frightened.

We spent the next day at home, taking turns to race to the shops for bottles and a cot and clothes and all manner of things. Frederic suggested a name for her, but it was so soon, and I needed to know her better. The baby slept, and then she didn't, and then she did, and by nightfall my body was an ocean of exhaustion. The day after that, I took the lead and suggested a trip to the park. Frederic scurried around packing a nappy, then two more, then another one into a laptop bag. We deliberated about sunscreen, not knowing if this baby (was she four months old? Five?) could yet have it applied to her delicate skin. As she lay on the rug, we googled *sunscreen babies rash prohibited?* Google was confusing. Between us we decided to water down a small amount of sunscreen with kettle-boiled water, gently rubbing it on her nose and cheeks. She glanced from me to Frederic.

'Have you seen her cheeks?' Frederic traced her pudgy jaw with his finger, catching a drop of cream before it fell.

'They're extraordinary,' I said. 'Like marble.'

Forty minutes later and we still had not left the house. Frederic strapped our new baby carrier around his body. He reached out to the baby who spat up and then the dog vomited on the top step so we turned and went back inside, Frederic saying, 'Our first outing!' very loudly. Dear Frederic. Is it possible I loved him even more? That was when I still thought love was finite, when I didn't know how it could expand to fit any vessel. I assumed that Frederic conferring love onto the baby meant less for me, a conviction that actually filled me with joy. I had taken up enough of him for too long. Here was a baby who would truly appreciate him. That made me feel lighter. In the hallway I took him by the arm. I said, 'You're right about her name.'

The baby glanced down, stuck one small fist in her mouth.

'That's her name.'

Frederic worked from home. He vowed to look at his days anew, to map the full twenty-four hours, to get his ten hours of work done at whatever time of the day, however it spread itself out around Lillian.

I didn't tell my colleagues at the library about her. I took one day off, then another, citing nothing specific because my boss didn't care and I never took time off. When I finally returned to work, it was a Wednesday. I lifted the box of animal puppets out of the cupboard with new vigour. I offered to run the morning storytime for toddlers. I felt my interest in each of these children grow. They shoved away their mothers' hands and wobbled over to pluck the puppets off my fingers.

Afterwards a woman with a child came over to borrow *Ghosts of the Tsunami* by Richard Lloyd Parry. I wanted to warn her that it might be too traumatic. For people with children – and that is what I was now – it was tempting but also dangerous to indulge in catastrophic thinking. To picture the specific and relentless calamities that might rain down on our offspring or sweep them away. Contaminate the air where our children breathed. But in the interests of doing my job, I scanned the woman's card and handed over the book. I thought of Lillian.

The next weekend, Frederic and I cancelled our plans. On Friday night we tucked her into bed, filled two glasses with wine and sat side by side at the kitchen table. We answered the paperwork the man from the department had sent, imagining Lillian's pleasing name settling on the ears of some jaded bureaucrat – or, if we were lucky, another *poet* bureaucrat – and filling that person with a happy idea of who Lillian might be, and the parents who loved her. Their approval was something I needed to know about. But beyond that, I needed to know that these pieces of paper would be filed away and then forgotten. That we had slipped through that zip in the universe one final time, with no-one coming after us.

I no longer cared what the women at work did with their spare time, or whether I was invited. There hadn't been talk of a group birthday dinner for months, and the thought of anything other than heading straight home filled me with anxiety. When I saw that I'd missed a call from the fertility doctor, I texted back, *We've adopted!* and blocked his number.

To my colleagues one morning while we sat with our packed lunches, I repeated, 'We've adopted!'

These people weren't fools. They knew this sort of stuff took a long time.

'There's a new department,' I said. 'It's very high up. It's all about fast-tracking.'

They were delighted for us. They wanted to know her name, and how well she slept. I told them Lillian's age, coming down definitively on five months. They made me promise to bring her in to the library as soon as possible, though I knew it was unlikely. After work I raced home. I unlocked our letterbox, and lying inside was an envelope from the department. I froze and called out to Frederic, who took it from me and started to ease it open, while I lifted Lillian to my face and took one of her cheeks gently between my lips. She recognised me, this woman whose mouth was on her skin, always.

'Shit,' I said. 'Please.' I used to be a believer, but no more. Not for years. Still: 'Please,' I said aloud, towards the sky. What would it take, this time around?

Sweet and docile Frederic was taking too long so I grabbed the envelope back. My fingers scrabbled at it. A single sheet of paper fell to the ground. Frederic picked it up and turned it around to show me. A departmental birth certificate with Lillian's beautiful name embossed in something close to gold.

Two weeks later Lillian was still safely with us and it grew hot. I put her down for a nap in her room with the fan on low. In the bathroom I took out some old strips of cloth from the medicine cabinet, steeped them in water then set them in the freezer. Afterwards I tied them around my wrists and my neck. I lay on the floor in our kitchen and pushed all thoughts of Lillian's mother away. I remembered my colleagues at the library, the women I worked with, and the way they tended to one another's fears about the fates of their families, how they propagated them.

When I heard my daughter cry, I undid the strips of cloth and went to her room. Inside her cot Lillian was on her back, her pink legs kicking up and out. When I found her on the beach, she had been as pale as driftwood.

The next day I came home and couldn't see Lillian or Frederic in the house. The dog followed me from room to room, getting tangled in my legs when I backed into her. I marched out through the laundry and into the backyard, where I spotted the pair of them seated along the fence next to the frangipani tree. I could almost see the secrets flowing between them. Tears welled behind my eyes, a feeling like gauze. There was no wind but the sky was hazy, and I had to squint against the glare. I watched them on the wooden bench. They were holding something between them. I took a few steps closer and saw that it was a long blade of grass, Frederic holding one end, Lillian pawing at the other. It was hard to believe they'd not spent their whole lives in this way: a diptych in the garden, leaning into each other like saints.

I barrelled over, propelled by my body's untightening. 'I didn't know where you were.'

I saw that I'd frightened her. Her face reddened and she cried at the loss of the grass, of the moment of peace with her dad.

'It's okay,' Frederic said to both of us. 'She's here.' He nodded, watching me closely.

'I was calling out. How did you not hear me?'

His eyes took in the back lawn and the short distance from the house. 'She's all right, aren't you? Everything's fine.'

She disappeared on a Sunday.

Sheets of rain elbowed the heat out of the air, steam rising from the hot bitumen. It had been a regular day for Lillian, ending in a late-afternoon nap. After an hour of silence, I looked in her crib and saw it empty. *Of course she's gone.* I laid my hand on the sheet, touching something gritty. When I brought my palm to my face, I saw that it was sand.

I searched for her under the cot, under the couch. I called her name. I checked in the bath. She hadn't started crawling, but maybe she'd magicked herself onto the low shelf in the pantry or beneath the clothesline. Through the rain, I felt my body fizzing and spitting. *I* was the hot bitumen. *I* was the scorched earth.

Robotic, or at least trying to be, I put the strips of cloth in the freezer and stood, waiting for them to be ready, looking at the fridge, at the phone number for the department we had stuck there. This was not a police matter, I could feel that in my bones. We had kidnapped that baby, but we'd forbidden ourselves to ever say that word.

I tied the cloth to my wrists and lay on the floor. When I turned my head, I saw a plastic toy boat upright beside the dishwasher. I started to cry. Frederic would be home soon, and the confluence of him returning and the cold bandages would surely calm me. One of us would know what to do.

Frederic could tell as soon as he saw my face. When I enlisted him to help, he came with me from room to room, watching as I turned over the doona and threw aside toiletries under the bathroom sink. He observed me carefully, like I was explosive. He told me that everything would work out. The dog was in a fit, running circles around Frederic's feet. 'Sit!' I cried. 'Dumb dog.'

She was barking at something, out beyond the front door. I opened it and watched the rain fall. 'See? Nothing.'

Frederic reached for my hand.

A voice came from the darkness. 'Hello?'

It was a man, his face streaked with rain, coming tentatively up the path to our door.

'Who is it?' I noticed the swell in my voice, my panic accelerating.

'I'm from the department,' he yelled out. 'Though they don't know I'm here. We spoke on the phone the night you found her.'

The bureaucrat. The poet.

'Do you know where she is?' Frederic asked. He gathered the dog in his arms. She was soggy and cold, but I understood my husband's need for her shivering, confused comfort.

'I can't tell you,' the poet replied.

'Yes, you can,' I said, striding out beyond the patio roof. The rain splattered my head, but I felt myself growing, like a plant. 'We won't say how we found out.'

'No, ma'am.'

'You told us we were in the clear.' I sobbed. I'd sobbed before, in moments of loss like this, but that hadn't been for months.

He smiled. 'Ah. But, you see, you told me *you'd* keep her safe.' The water had drenched his shirt, which was white and turned up at the cuffs. His tie hung loose. I suspected he'd ditched a jacket somewhere. In my head went the thud: *Lillian Lillian Lillian*. Her name was a sound drawn through trees, a bow across a violin.

'Perhaps,' he said, 'they have reclassified the definition of wilderness.'

'*Wilderness*?' Frederic said. Maybe he had not given this word a second thought. But I'd kept it as close as my spine.

'It used to include beaches. Babies found on beaches. Now perhaps it doesn't.'

'How can they change it like that?' I shrieked. But of course they could do what they liked. The tide came in and the tide went out.

And our Lillian, she was pure alchemy, washing up on the sand. 'That's beyond cruel.'

He wiped away what I was saying with his hand. 'It's not for me to assess. These decisions come from high up. We get no warning. She'll be safe with the department.'

The floodlight above the path cast a shadow over the bureaucrat's face like clouds on a flat, pale ocean.

'She is *ours*,' I said.

'Sir, please,' Frederic added. He grappled with the dog, held her as tightly as he could, while her eyes sharpened from one of us to the other. If we let the dog go now, could she put her snout to the sodden ground before the clues washed away? Or had the dog already lost the scent?

The bureaucrat–poet seemed to be backing away. The day was turning. Darkness thickened, and with it all this heavy rain and unknown strangers' hands upon my baby who was out in the naked night. Something in me unfastened. Not strange at all how that orca kept her calf with her while she churned through the Pacific: two points, nose to nose. As if you'd ever let go.

'Why did you come?' I yelled.

He stopped and took a handkerchief from his pocket, wiped his face, ran it through his hands. 'You wanted a baby,' he said softly. 'Something must have gone wrong. A loss like this is usually the cause of an internal investigation. But that's classified. I don't *know* why she was taken. I know ...'

'Yes?' Frederic said.

The poet had said too much. He shut up like a clam. Then: 'Did you know that Ben Jonson lost his daughter, then his first son, then his next son, too. He wrote: "Farewell, thou child of my right hand, and joy."'

I felt an enormous slink of fear. 'We'll do anything,' I said. I had forgotten how to exist and who I was before Lillian. I hated the house behind me. I would never go back inside. Frederic and I had done this together. We shared Lillian and, for the first time properly, we shared each other. It was alchemy, too, how we had gone from one thing to another. I needed to appeal to the poet in this man. 'We ... Do you know why we named her Lillian?'

He shook his head, and I saw sympathy there. I saw that he himself was probably a father. He certainly looked weary.

'It was the name of the boat,' I told him. '*Lillian*. Painted on the side. And it was under her.'

'Under her?'

I nodded. 'She was sort of on a piece of wood. The one that had her name on it. Frederic went back to find it, but it was gone.'

'Wait.' The poet moved closer up the path, one of his hands held up in query. 'She was on the water?'

'On the piece of wood,' Frederic said, sounding strange. 'Right at the water's edge.' Something in Frederic's voice was seeking something in the man.

Under the surface a tide was changing. The bureaucrat glanced towards the street behind him. 'I spy a little bit of hope.'

I couldn't breathe. 'Yes?'

'Would you like me to drive you?'

His car was a ten-year-old sedan, a dull silver with half-a-dozen faded bumper stickers on the back window. The Beach Boys were playing. The windscreen wipers thudded a contrary rhythm to the song. Frederic, usually so talkative and animated as a passenger, was silent.

We drove without stopping. The man took roundabouts gently

as we headed north out of our estate and up along the coast. All the traffic lights were green. To our right, the ocean shattered on the dark beach.

Finally, Frederic asked, 'Where are you taking us?'

The poet cleared his throat. 'You see, our department is small. We are overworked. We make judgements based on the information given. You must understand, a *beach* is a wilderness,' he said, lifting a hand off the steering wheel and pointing towards the coast, 'but a vessel is *thalassic*. That the child arrived by boat – that comes under the purview of a different department. Someone must have worked out she was not a Wilderness Find and passed it on. I know where we'll find her.'

He turned the car into a road – we'd been the only vehicle for kilometres – that became a complicated network of roundabouts and dead ends in a commercial estate I'd never been to. I thought of returning to our empty house, empty-handed. The horror prowled inside me. The poet slowed when he reached the end of the street, pulled a card from the glovebox and swiped it on a reader out the window. He turned off the engine, and I saw that we were in the car park of a three-storey building lit by the floodlights we had triggered.

'They'll be pleased you're here.'

Whatever was inside that building was invisible to me in the night-time behind two glass doors, and I felt myself start to shiver, and then I couldn't stop. Frederic put his arm around me. My arms ached to hold her.

We went inside. A modest foyer, a sign, a woman, a desk – almost empty, just a single folder and pen. The woman stood and came round to us. She was petite, elegant in a grey dress and heels. She had black eyes and she smiled when she spoke, her eyes crinkling at the edges. She introduced herself as a retired ship's captain, now a senior public servant in the Department of Maritime Affairs. 'So, you are responsible for the child?'

'Yes,' Frederic and I said together. We hadn't let each other go.

'Come with me.' She led the poet first, then the two of us, down a corridor that smelt like a hospital, with lights along the skirting boards. Her heels clicked as our bureaucrat loped beside her, one step to her two.

'Here,' the captain said, stopping before a doorway. 'But I must warn you.' And she explained the shipwreck, how Lillian had been its sole survivor. I must have gotten a look in my eyes because Frederic put his face close to mine and gave me a gentle shake, and I understood that to faint right now would be a bad idea. It was a room where the bodies were laid out on tables. Six long mounds covered in plastic. Frederic reached for my hand. One of those bodies had held Lillian in the ocean of her belly. Cells dividing and dividing, that alchemy again in a quiet and unknown space.

I paused to stare at the bodies for only as long as it took to remind myself that in this department I would take what was mine. For years I had been friendless because I was selfish. Here, I would do it again. Here, my selfishness had grown – my world was three people now. Into that sorrowful room I sent a prayer and a promise. I would put their baby above everything else. My heart quickened. I was learning all sorts of things about myself.

We came to the next room. I stood longer, waiting to see what the objects from the boat spelt out for me in a way I'd never allow the bodies to. A table stood inside the door with things arranged on it – *lovingly*, I thought, watching the woman's back as she trotted off ahead, wondering if this curating, too, was part of her job.

There was a diamond-shaped plate as white as bone; shards of glass and also one perfect tumbler, waiting for a refill; gold and silver coins; yellow rubber thongs; a backpack pummelled thin; a hat shaped, curiously, like a boat. And at the centre was the piece of timber that had delivered Lillian to us, her name curled across it in ribbon blue.

I heard footsteps. I turned. And then, there she was, quite suddenly, in the arms of the captain.

Our Lillian, a round and bright creature, fighting to liberate a hand from the white cloth that bound her. Half a day older. Mere hours after the silly dog hadn't warned me there was a retired captain roaming our house. Somehow more like me, looking even more like she was ours.

The captain motioned to the rooms that held the bodies and the dinner plates picked clean by salt and sand. 'You've seen that the child's parents have perished. We have processed her, and the orphan is yours.' Then she handed her to us.

The poet and the captain grinned, but I felt far away from them both.

I found Lillian's eyes and brushed her brow with my fingers. She wriggled against my chest.

'Lillian,' I said.

Frederic covered his eyes, beginning to cry.

When he lifted his hands, we watched each other as the joy poured over us like steam.

NIGHT BLINDNESS

1947 | GERTY THERESA CORI | PHYSIOLOGY OR MEDICINE

Prize motivation: 'for their discovery of the course of the catalytic conversion of glycogen'

AT SUNSET GERTY STEADIED HERSELF on the deck and gazed out to the Atlantic. She wondered what she would miss from home. America had mountains to climb and ski – a professor at the institute in Buffalo had posted them photographs in a blue envelope. Pictures of meadows and mountains to compensate for the ones they'd grown to love in Vienna and in Prague. It was nice to know there were people who wanted them to be happy in their new home.

A tremendous wind found her and battered at her neck and wrists. She pulled her coat around her, walking the length of the great ship and smoking. She'd packed enough cigarettes for the trip. She wrote letters to Carl, not knowing which ones would reach him before they'd see each other again. In one of his letters – for six months he'd been a beautiful and diligent letter writer – Carl said he'd seen a girl at the institute who reminded him of her, a comment she tried to recall cheerily. It was good that her new husband was settling in. Good that dozens more were getting to know his calmness, his gentleness, his curiosity. The girl smoked Lucky Strikes, like all the American girls did.

Ten days on a ship. The same faces. Gerty had never before been this *still* so she led her brain in experiments to pass the time. She carried a notebook and a pen to the aft part of the saloon promenade deck where they were permitted. Girls, little twins, ran laps when they escaped from their parents. Some days, Gerty gathered objects and laid them out on the sisters' usual route to see which objects tempted them to slow, and for how long. A cup, an empty can, a red pencil from the dining room. She observed which girl stopped first, before both squatted using their fat, solid knees, their bottoms almost touching the deck. Boarding in Rotterdam, a young man had brought an exotic parrot coloured green, yellow and blue, which he kept in his cabin during the day only to take out at night in a cage that he held up like a lantern. One evening Gerty watched one of its feathers fall from the cage to the deck and she held her breath to see who else would notice. She moved as quickly as she could till she was standing right beside the feather, and then bent down to seize it. In her cabin she laid it on her iron bed and twisted it in her fingers. The gold and green shimmered.

The next afternoon at dusk Gerty pinned the feather down at its most delicate end with a stone. She chose a bench where she sat alone. Somewhere beneath her, beside her, all around, the steam turbines pulsed and shook the body of the ship. Teenage boys in shirts and ties kicked a ball. Finally the two girls came into sight, huddled against the wind in the arms of an old man, their faces turned to each other across the expanse of his broad chest. After a long time, the man set the sisters down and they spied the feather. One removed the stone, which she brought close to her face to inspect. The other picked up the feather. The stone was dropped, the feather reached for, not handed over. Screeching till the man came to bundle them both up. It was the only object they ever stole from the deck. Gerty made a note in her book.

Each night she sat in the dining saloon with her new friends, Mrs Novy and her sixteen-year-old niece, Minnie. They were her cabinmates in their third-class stateroom. 'I was named after a warship,' Gerty told Minnie, when they first met. Two tables across, Gerty saw the twin sisters squashing pieces of bread on their plates with the full force of their chubby hands, then posting them daintily into their mouths.

Gerty pressed open her notebook on the white linen next to her place setting. She liked to sketch and caption the dishes of food they were served. *Boiled striped bass with creamed horseradish. Salmi of duckling with green peas. Calf's sweetbread à la Maréchale.* Mrs Novy watched her, sometimes pointing out when Gerty got the spelling wrong, or made a mistake with the shading of the blueberries.

For Carl, was what Gerty mostly thought. *To show him, to compare notes in case he did the same thing six months ago.* But also to record the ingredients and dishes she might try to make, where her future self could go to a market and search for green peas in their shells. To see if, in New York, you could buy a pound of calf's liver and then cook it for your husband.

A waiter came to their side, and Mrs Novy and Minnie shifted their spoons to make room. The three women nodded at the tall blond man. One could never be sure if the waiters onboard spoke Dutch or Danish or French. Gerty gave the waiter a hearty, '*Dank u wel.*'

He set a bowl in her place. His cap of soft golden hair reminded her of Carl's.

'*Tak!*' she said, slipping her pen between her fingers, eyeing the dessert.

Orange ice cream and gooseberry tart.

In anatomy class she had been the only woman, the only Jew. On her first day her instinct was to keep quiet. But her mother's voice, and the voices of her mother's rowdy, bookish friends rang in her ears: *Speak up, girl!* She pictured them lounging while a record played, holding drinks like bulbs of light in their hands, urging her on as they dropped ash onto the carpet.

Carotid artery, subclavian artery, cranial neural crest, the medulla oblongata. Muscle and bone. Her own innervation when she and Carl met, when she spoke up, when she made herself known to him across a table in the laboratory. Drawing him out. Speaking up. Making him laugh. The vibration in her larynx followed by deliberate touches of her lips, teeth, tongue.

Later, there were the notches of his vertebrae as he banked beneath the sheet. Later still, the war in which the babies, the mothers, the farmers, the school teachers, the aldermen, the painters, the postmen, the soldiers and the sergeants all went hungry. After none of them had enough to eat, there was – for malnourished Gerty – an anatomical interest in her eye. She took notes. She learnt about keratomalacia, xerophthalmia, night blindness.

The ship crashed through the ocean. It followed a line on a map that was taking her away from Vienna and its pencilled-in, light-filled sky. In Vienna there were trams and horses, cars and trains. Couples stepped into the street. Wrinkled, bronzed women sold flowers in baskets outside Café de l'Europe. She and Carl had gone to Wurstelprater and waved at the families crammed into the miniature train before it ducked under the bridge. They bought tickets for the Ferris wheel and the roller coaster. A sign at the very top said: *Sitzen bleiben! Hüte festhalten!* right before the carriage plunged them down into the water. Children crowded around the mini puppet theatre, and Gerty tried to remember the names of the puppets, and their agony and arguments, what their cottony thrashes were all about, so that she could tell her little patients at the children's hospital when she returned to them the next day.

At breakfast Mrs Novy slid her bowl to one side and took Gerty's hands in hers. Mrs Novy smelt floury, like bread. She bent her large, plaited head towards Gerty. Mrs Novy had made this journey before. This time she was taking Minnie to New York, where they would both stay for good. There would be plenty of jobs for her niece in a year or two when she was ready, in a factory in Brooklyn or as a cook in one of the fancy hotels. Big sugar refineries lined the rivers; busy dockyards were filled with men. Her niece would make a fine seamstress. Because Mrs Novy had been onboard before, she spoke about the ship as though it had been her design. She knew the shortest routes from deck to deck; she knew what each clanging pipe meant, and whether the soup Gerty was about to eat was the worst on the menu, or the best.

Mrs Novy asked, 'Are you leaving your mother and father behind?'

Gerty nodded. 'He worked in a sugar refinery, too. My father.'

'Perhaps you will reunite in America.'

After all of Mrs Novy's talk about funnels and masts, about steam turbines, about everything she apparently knew of the great ocean liner, Gerty feared that doughy Mrs Novy saying this had just plunged her into a future where she would never see her mother or father again.

On their final night onboard they met for a stroll before supper. Gerty slid a cigarette from its packet and ducked into a doorway so the match would take. Mrs Novy had never asked what she did for work; Gerty had met plenty of people like her before, although in her experience it was usually men who never asked. Despite this, she was fond of the woman who, with her matronly skirts, thick waist and stockings corrugated with wrinkles, reminded her of precisely none of her mother's glamorous friends. On the day they met she asked Gerty what her wedding had been like and what they had eaten afterwards. She pointed to the book open on Gerty's mattress and asked her to sketch a picture of her wedding gown. At the very least, knowing one extra person in New York might be useful.

They reached the stern, where Gerty smoked at the railing. Lights were coming on across the ship. Dinner would be waiting.

'Shall we go back?' Mrs Novy asked.

'Let's stay a moment,' Gerty said, wanting another cigarette before the meal.

The colossal silver ocean thundered below.

Gerty said, 'Sometimes when you are standing in the dark talking to someone, you say things you wouldn't necessarily say in the daylight. Don't you think? That the dark, it is sometimes illuminating?'

'Are you worried about your husband?' Mrs Novy asked.

Gerty turned to face the woman. 'Worried in what way?'

'About what you will think of each other after six months.'

'Not at all. It's gone like *that.*' She clicked her fingers and the cigarette came loose from her right hand. She watched it for a second, falling through the wind, to the water.

'Good,' Mrs Novy said, 'because you are not like other women I've met. I told Minnie that she'll meet lots of women like you in America.'

One more cigarette. Gerty thought of the warm dining room, the pink-faced waiters bearing plates of beef and potatoes. She was cold. And suddenly ravenous.

HYPEROBJECT

1963 | MARIA GOEPPERT MAYER | PHYSICS

*Prize motivation: 'for their discoveries
concerning nuclear shell structure'*

1.

There aren't many of us left. And I don't mean people who could do shorthand – now, that's a dying art. A dead one, in fact. When's the last time anyone ever wrote you something in shorthand? Well, it used to be a valuable skill, highly sought after. I was a typist, I could do shorthand, I worked the switch. I lived in a dormitory with women who did jobs like these. Matron's rules were simple, and they reflected the rules of the whole place. A diary would have been unthinkable, but I've always had a good memory.

2.

You want to be as smart as you can, my father told me when I was a girl in Colorado. As brave as you can. As trustworthy and as honest. You can never be too much of any of those things. I had hoped to become an engineer, although there weren't many women doing that. But I had ambition, you see. So when the ad came up, I said goodbye to my mother and my father, to my older brother who adored me, and I moved out to Tennessee.

3.

Well, the place was full of mud, and my first thought was that I had to get on the next train out. It didn't seem glamorous or exciting, not one bit. I was all set to take off when I saw a row of women emerging from between the gates. How sharp they looked, how important, like their brains were going a mile a minute thinking of vital things. I thought long and hard about what was back home for me in Colorado. I signed up for a dorm room, put away my things in the dreary wardrobe, and I stayed the first night and then the next, and the next.

4.

There wasn't much to do so most nights we hung about in each other's rooms for company. There was a lonely hearts section in the little newspaper. A few people worked on the paper for the town, putting in puns at every opportunity. The page was called 'Atom Seeks Eve' and it ran on Thursdays, maybe to give people time enough to have a date by Saturday night.

'Ever thought about this?' my friend Margery asked. She prodded the paper.

'For me? What would I say?'

'My cousin in Grand Rapids met her boyfriend through one of these. You just say how old you are, and what you like doing, and what you want in a man.'

The cat inched into the room and came for my legs, threading her long grey body around my ankles. The cat was new. She started up one night, mewling outside the dormitory fire escape. I waited for someone else to hop up and give her a kick to get going, but no-one did. So I went out there in my nightgown and slippers, and the cat gave me such a look that I brought her into my room. I shut the door and put my hands into the crooks of her bony forelegs and lifted her to my face.

We were allowed hotplates in our bedrooms. I had a desk and a couple of ferns. The wardrobe was tall and skinny and wonky; Oak Ridge and everything in it was built pretty quickly, from what I've heard. I opened the wardrobe and moved aside my heels. I laid down a big soft purse my brother bought me years ago, and the cat surveyed it, plonked right down and went to sleep.

I didn't want a boyfriend, I remember thinking that firmly. I remember this moment – Margery touching the tip of her finger to the tip of her tongue, wetting it. I remember her eagerness for me to sign up, something she was never going to do, for me to provide the drama. Our lives were fairly empty. But my dorm room was home. Others whined about the heating or how strict Matron was about curfew, but I figured some man would just as likely set a curfew for me in my own house. Before places like Oak Ridge and Los Alamos, some of the physicists, the women, couldn't even get a job. Who else would accept secretive offers – to produce a bomb, no less – other than women who for five, ten years had done work for free? I'm cynical, my daughters tell me. It's my son who believes me when I tell him this, doesn't make me feel like I'm making it up. He knows what men are capable of.

5.

We kept our mouths shut and didn't post letters to our families back home containing anything they weren't supposed to know. What did I think was happening there? What did I think we were doing? It's hard to say. I knew this wasn't like a gold drive, or one for silver or tin. We weren't out in some desert, asking grannies for their wedding trinkets to turn into shells. The war effort felt so enormous; its reach was everywhere. It isn't like today when a war can be going on and nobody talks about it. This was all there was. So I thought my work had something to do with weapons, maybe plans for a submarine. It was hard work, our days were long, but the work pleased me, down to my bones. I couldn't imagine returning to a life where I would be bored.

People got up to all sorts. Ridiculous things the boys did in their hours off. They once moved their supervisor's car in the mud. Five or six of them just picked it up and shifted it to a different parking lot and it took him half a day to find it. Well, those things were pure joy. Mischief like that, we got away with. I watched those boys, and their pride in what they'd done.

6.

Then one night – you'll know which one – the street outside my dormitory was silent until a sheet of cheers came across the cold air like a tablecloth pulled over a table, and I soon found out that a bomb had been dropped. I bent towards the floor and I began to pray. This wasn't new for me. I was a big believer in praying, still am. For hours there was singing and laughing. Hurrahs sent up to the sky. I imagined folks kissing, all that going on right outside my window. Some lonely hearts had found each other, and why shouldn't they? Love and war. I heard shoes galloping down the hallway. On an ordinary day, that was not permitted – Matron didn't allow running.

One huge party, which I didn't begrudge them.

And yet.

I laid my head on the floor and cried. With the tender part of my forehead cooling bit by bit, and the noises from outside scaling higher and higher into the cloudless sky, I remembered something absurd: I needed to buy pressed powder. I needed to buy soap. My mother would finally know what I'd been doing out here, and I waited for her to call me and ask.

7.

It's not like nowadays, when someone might ask, *What are we here for? What are we doing? Where's all this leading?* No-one was demanding answers.

The government, you have to understand, stuck up eviction papers on doors, took people's land in New Mexico, arranged for cheques to be left at the post office. Gave them a month to move out, sometimes less. It was a different time. Nobody liked leaving everything behind, but they did it. Losing their peach farms, their family stock, going who knows where, if they even had somewhere to go, bewildered, whatever, but you did what you were told. I'm not saying it's right, I'm saying that's all they were offered.

8.

Three years later and I was back in damn Colorado, not doing much. One afternoon I was painting stones in the sun, arranging faces onto the smooth flat sides to make into pet rocks with my brother's little boy. Who loved me. Five times up to the house for buttons and glue and ribbon, telling him to wait there. Then back to the shade of my parents' front lawn. A man was coming up the road towards us to ask if we had a telephone he could borrow. I saw that man and I fell in love.

9.

I look at photos of myself now, although never when I'm alone – nostalgia is a one-way trip, Daniel was fond of saying.

No, when I get those photos out I'm doing it for the grandkids. Who are egging me on. Shouldn't it be the other way round? That the oldies have to con the young ones into sitting side by side on a couch with the albums laid out flat? Not in my experience. Which one gets to hold the photo album, that's a fight. Who gets to turn the page, that's another. I'm certainly flattered, but it knocks me around while they're here – Ronnie is twelve, Christopher is nine, Vivi is eight – and I gratefully shut the door after they've gone. They're voracious, that's what takes it out of me. Photos, yes, especially Daniel and me on our wedding day, they love that one. But then it's on to the next thing. All things are equally interesting to them. When I was young I feel as though I liked four things, maybe five. Not kids these days. Everything is *theirs*. Everything holds something they can admire, absorb, take.

So, these photos. I have a few from Oak Ridge, clippings from the newspaper. A piece out of the lonely hearts, which of course Ronnie and Christopher and Vivi think is priceless, think is completely old-fashioned. Which it is. Don't people search for love these days? Isn't it still the biggest thing there is? But I don't say that to my grandkids while they gobble the cake their parents have sent along. Crumbs gather in the line formed from their calf muscles folded back into their thighs. They let me touch their legs. They get a kick out of my squeezing them. The firmness. That's a thing I can't get over. And in the photographs I see how young I was, when indeed I thought I was old. How vain I was, how frightened of ageing. I thought I was old when I was actually very, very young.

Beautiful creatures, my grandchildren unfold from sitting and drift away from me. The big album bounces on the couch with the force of their leaving. Then they're off, whatever they can find in my house. They know I watch the clock while they're here. But they're guileless, and whatever I do is nutty. They think I'm adorable. And I find myself so fond of them, and the shapes of their backs. They're hopping from foot to foot at the sliding door while they decide what's next. The t-shirts they wear are stretched across their shoulder blades and I think: love is enormous.

10.

Years after Oak Ridge, and years after Daniel had died, when I lived alone in an apartment in Santa Fe, I foolishly chipped a tooth trying to prise open a glass bottle and I had to take an emergency trip to the dentist. There, in the waiting room, I read a story in *National Geographic* about the women who worked at Los Alamos during the Manhattan Project. Some of them signed a petition – this all came out later, you see. The petition set about begging the government to demonstrate a prototype of the bomb to the government of Japan as a warning. *Before* they zoomed over to Hiroshima, in case the whole mess could have been avoided. But they'd ignored these women – of course they had – and all the other petitioners.

I sat in the waiting room, in the comfortable chair. I nursed the bright pain in my jaw, looking out the window towards the foothills, and I closed the magazine. How strange, then, that those women still felt something like triumph go through their bodies when they saw the destruction they had created.

FROST

1964 | DOROTHY CROWFOOT HODGKIN | CHEMISTRY

Prize motivation: 'for her determinations by X-ray techniques of the structures of important biochemical substances'

I THOUGHT YOU WOULD BE A BOY, but no matter. I will teach you how to make a dovetail joint. Let me teach you how to spit and swim and how to run faster than you thought you knew how. When you're older, I'll show you how to climb the sycamore, where to put your feet, and how to build a fire in the corner of the yard. I will teach you how to wring a chicken's neck. I will teach you how to catch a snowflake on your tongue and spot an enemy plane. The war is pretty much over now, but if you ever get caught outside in an air raid, find a respectable house where the mother will give you a cup of tea and a biscuit while you wait for it to be over. Occasionally, when there's a wrinkled aunt in town, you will get taken for a special meal and you must remember to enjoy every moment. Do not burp out loud, little sister. If you need to wee, put up your hand and ask, 'May I leave the table?' If you're hurrying to get back to the special meal, wet your fingertips slightly so they think for sure you've washed them.

When you're old enough to go to school, you'll find that you enjoy it, not just the books and reading but getting into small scraps of trouble. But most of all you will teach yourself how to paint.

Now, little sister. As you grow you will be asked to paint famous people. Once, you drew me, do you remember this? We were stacked up together in the shed and I had the axe in my hand, which I knew how to use because someone had taught me. And you took off inside and came back with paper and pencil and a biscuit because you must have known I'd need to keep steady for a bit and would need distracting. The shed was pale timber with a grey roof. Once, we fashioned pins and carved a wooden ball to make a game out there too, but the pins got wet and grew kind of warped, so most likely we moved on to the next thing quick smart, you taking your cue from your dear older brother that there are plenty of things to do and people to see and tricks to try. There was nothing in you that said you would only ever look at something in a single way.

One day you will go to Warwickshire to paint a portrait of Dorothy Hodgkin, the famous scientist. It will be early in the year 1985, Christmas just gone, people are drowsy and feeling spongy all over, tinsel still hung. The chimneys are pulling smoke up from hearths into the air. The prime minister will be determined to break the miners' strike, and you will make a note to ask about Thatcher because you know that, years ago, she was one of Dorothy's pupils. Although perhaps there are no questions left to ask about this, and personally you do not care about the rimy prime minister or how her mind works. You see the village of Ilmington from a distance: the spire of the church and the neat thatched roofs. The snow is thick on the ground, and mist rises up from behind limestone buildings pretty with black trim. The fields are frozen hard. The only sounds are your boots crunching against the stones, pressing down on the meadow foxtail as you cross over to the professor's cottage.

She's a grand lady. A bony, regal presence. A gentle intellect towers within her. She leads you through to her office, which overlooks a pair of salad-green oaks. Quickly, your heart vaults. The light in this room is better than good. In photographs of her as a younger woman, her eyes are expressive, dark, almost mournful, although you've learnt not to misattribute thoughts and feelings to your subjects.

But it's true she was beautiful. Attentive. Curious.

Oh, see, little sister, you cannot help it!

'All right,' the professor says. 'You tell me what you would like me to do.' While she talks she grips the high back of the chair. So you suggest she sits and works on something, while you set up and perhaps take some photographs to start. You know she is a woman who works and works. The desk in her office has stacks of paper, a stapler, some fine black markers. A tall bookshelf is behind her. In it are folders with spines of white, lilac, blue and red. The professor is dressed in a blouse and cardigan knitted thickly, in a colour like waves. Her hair is snowy bright and fine as filament with bare patches of skull beneath.

You drew Mum after she'd died, and years later you will sketch one of your lovers – also dead. If I'd had a brother he wouldn't have done that. Oh, no. But a sister. You taught yourself to do precisely what you wished.

You open a sketchbook onto your lap to make some preliminary marks. 'Yes, if that's comfortable,' you say. 'If you could show me how you use this room, the sorts of things you do while you're here.'

Well, there is nothing unnatural about the professor and she moves as though you are not there – a dream for a painter like you. From shelf to paper to pen, opening folders and holding her hands in a patch of sunlight. She drops a pen and reaches down for it before you can help. Minutes pass.

'You're rather good at this, Professor.'

'Am I?'

'You're not messing about with your hair or asking if I'm finished yet,' you tell her. 'That's better than most.'

The only sounds are the scratch of your pencil on sketchbook and Dorothy shuffling papers about.

'And Maggie Thatcher?' you finally ask.

'Mrs Thatcher, yes.'

'You taught her?'

'At Somerville, a very long time ago. Most people want to know what she was like.' Dorothy peers through thick glasses.

'Not me,' you say, laughing, and she seems to enjoy this.

After an hour or so, you take a mug of tea and a cigarette out to the back garden. The cold air is sharp and hushed, giving you a good chance to rinse your brain and wonder about the next step. Hard to think inside a house that is full to the brim with heating. You light the cigarette, imagining you're giving the professor a chance to rest, maybe use the loo. But there she is, coming out the side door, into the freezing yard. She motions towards the cigarette, and you think, *Oh, fuck, she disapproves.* But actually she's making conversation: for years it's been difficult for her to hold objects in her fingers.

'Your hands are lovely,' the professor says. 'Do they ever cramp up?'

'I'd have to chop them off if they did,' you say. Oh, a great woozy puff of smoke into your lungs. Better than tea, better than biscuits, better than running loops in the backyard with your dear older brother coming after you with a dead mouse he found, you squealing your head off, loving it all.

Soon it is time to go. Quick kiss on the cheek and the professor rubs your hands gently. You will of course need to return to the house to finish the painting – sometimes your subjects are surprised at this. So a proper thank you and then a goodbye, followed by a brisk race back to the cottage you've rented to the north of the village. Hills and meadows are frosted on all sides. Sure, it's only been a few days but there it is: a feeling that niggles at the back of your mind like a shell underfoot. You miss the ocean. Remember how we took it in turns to go on rides at the fair at Frinton-on-Sea? Remember that time you toddled into the waves and kept on walking? Mum had to race in and drag you out, calling you daft.

Thirty-five years somehow slip by, in the way time does. You still love walking where you shouldn't, ploughing into waves. You're older, yes, still doing as you please, still on the fags. You're taking a long walk with one of your friends from way, way back, and she mentions insulin. She natters away at you on this hard-for-your-heart walk along the beach. The word insulin comes from the Latin for *island*. You gaze out to the water and imagine an island. The waves are too cold for skinny-dipping, and you're too tired today to paint them. You get tired easily these days.

Insulin.

A fact loosens itself from your brain: you remember the bony, regal presence; the towering intellect; the expressive eyes. How you painted her with an insulin model close beside her on the desk – a kind of memento mori. What that woman discovered about insulin took her thirty-five years. Thirty-five! And now computers can do all that in days, probably.

With your strong and steady hands – the ones she thought

were lovely – you motion for your friend to slow the hell down, thinking that nothing will ever speed up the time it takes to paint a portrait. To sculpt something with your hands. It takes as long as it takes and it always has, always will.

STOCKHOLM

1977 | ROSALYN YALOW | PHYSIOLOGY OR MEDICINE

*Prize motivation: 'for the development of
radioimmunoassays of peptide hormones'*

OUT OF THE FREEZING WIND and into the lobby of the Grand Hotel Stockholm, the woman walks past the front desk and the men smoking cigars in high-backed chairs. Towards the elevators, and it's all nautical paintings and a twenty-foot Christmas tree strung with crimson apples and tiny flags. She has never been in a place this beautiful. At the bank of elevators a porter nods at her and presses the button. She decides to give herself over to being treated in this way, for the weekend. She travels to the third floor and fishes the key out of her pocket. When she unlocks their hotel suite, she sees that the housekeeper has been.

She opens the curtains. Evening outside reveals this foreign country – lights twinkle in restaurants and bars across the lake, the icy Baltic Sea out beyond the harbour. Even at this hour, bicycles sail past and cars on the street below edge forward in the coal-black night, where her husband is out walking, not yet done strolling after their rich, late lunch. His suit, pressed shirt and snowy white bow tie hang on a brass hook. Beneath one window is a chaise longue upholstered in a fabric as soft as a baby blanket. The woman removes her shoes and slings her handbag over a bedpost then lies for a time on the cream-and-gold comforter. The room smells of flowers, which are arranged in vases scattered throughout the bedroom, in one corner of the writing desk and even on the marble basin in the bathroom. She rises and unzips the cloth-bag hanging in her wardrobe. She runs a hand down the silk blouse and long peacock-blue skirt she plans to wear to the ceremony tomorrow. The vest, with its gold thread, looks regal and she delights in it. This was what she wanted to wear. Not an evening gown. She unpacks the bolo tie and the pearl earrings that her daughter loves. She takes the jewellery and places it in a dish on the dresser. Facing the mirror, grinning, she claps her hands.

The telephone rings. She thinks of her husband hurrying from street to street in the unfamiliar and freezing city. It is a safe city, she tells herself quickly, and he's wrapped in that enormous coat. But, still, telephone calls startle her. Her children are far away. She shudders.

'Hello?'

'Mrs Yalow, I'm sorry to disturb, but there's a girl at the desk. She's wondering if you might have time to speak with her, just briefly.'

'Oh,' she says and scans the room for her shoes and handbag. 'All right. I'll be down in a moment.'

The concierge directs her to a young woman seated at a modest pair of chairs in a nook against the wall. He brings over two coffees, which he sets on the small table between them.

The girl is Lena, and she is nervous.

'I love your outfit,' Mrs Yalow says.

Lena jumps on this, explaining, in a meandering way, in that beautiful accent, how she made the dress herself, on her mother's sewing machine. She shifts the emerald-green fabric across her knees – something for her to do with her hands, Mrs Yalow thinks. Lena is a student at Karolinska Institute, right here in Stockholm, and yesterday she asked her physics professor's advice: should she come to the Grand Hotel and try to meet a Nobel winner?

'And the answer was yes?'

'He said yes.' Lena smiles.

A trolley passes, pushed by a porter in black trousers and coat. Mrs Yalow stirs her coffee, waits for the girl to speak.

'You injected *yourself* with the radioactive-tagged insulin,' Lena says, 'to see if it would work?'

Mrs Yalow nods. 'It isn't that unusual. You might find, if you continue with your studies, you'll have a desire to make things work, no matter what.'

'You have had such an extraordinary life.'

Mrs Yalow touches her forehead and then points up, over her shoulder in the general direction of her hotel suite, where her suitcase is open on the bed. 'Would you believe a man wrote me before I came here, saying he works in the movies? He thinks my life would make a good film.'

The girl lets out a soft *ha* in amazement. 'What are you going to do? Are you going to say yes?'

'I haven't had time to think about it. He might be mistaken. He might think there's more to it than there is.' She laughs and sips her coffee.

It isn't, in fact, the first letter, but the third. The man is persistent, and it's lucky for him she finds persistence admirable. She has no idea how these things work but, when his first letter arrived rubberbanded with other mail on her desk, she wrote a reply containing what she thought was a polite yet firm no. Less than a month later, the man replied – enthusiastically, urgently – as though she had said yes. She and Sol had never patented radioimmunoassay. Perhaps this man thought they had, and that she was now wealthy. Maybe she was being taken for a ride. But the return address was for Calabasas, and movies were made out there all the time.

The girl smooths down the front of her dress and leans forward. 'At one point, you were the only woman in a faculty of four hundred.'

'That's right.'

'But you often found it hard to get work.'

'Yes, for many years.'

'Despite your qualifications.'

Mrs Yalow sets a finger on the table. She prods its surface *here*, then *there*, traces a jagged line in the space between the two spots. 'I just took different routes to get there.'

'And you went back to work one week after your son was born.'

'Yes,' she says, smiling at the image of her sleeping baby in his basket, and the different scents from her new life mixing for the first time, there in her laboratory. 'I was nursing so of course he had to come with me.'

Lena reminds her of her own daughter. A bit younger perhaps.

'How old are you?' she asks, because she doesn't like to make guesses.

'Nineteen. I'll be twenty next month.'

Mrs Yalow's hand shakes a little when she returns the cup to its saucer. 'What an exciting age. A terrific time.'

Nearby, a door sweeps open and through it walks her husband. She is filled with fondness for the man, affection as high and bright as the atrium. His cheeks are ruddy, and his coat – that great tan hulking thing he's had for fifteen years – is draped over his arm.

He must have worked up such a pace to digest their late lunch with its cheeses, the potato pancakes, the never-ending bread and jam, that somewhere along the way he felt the need to remove the coat.

Quickly, as though she can sense Mrs Yalow's attention splitting, Lena asks, 'Do you have any advice for me?'

'Work hard,' she replies, rising.

Lena doesn't smile.

Mrs Yalow spreads her hands out. 'Is there more to it than that?' She's waving now, trying to get her husband's attention, without being too loud, in a place like this.

Lena stands too and reaches for her coat hanging over the back of her chair. 'Do you have any specific advice for women, and all the demands on our lives that we must have?'

'Find somebody good to be by your side.' Mrs Yalow holds out her hand for shaking. 'Now. You tell me: what should I do about the movie man?'

Lena brightens. 'Oh, I love movies. You should say yes.'

What would Sol say? How wonderful it would be if she could speak to her lab partner again, this December evening in this glorious hotel. Not the ghost of him, but the real him, and get his advice. Sol, now five years gone after twenty years in the lab together. Sol, a genius, obviously, and capable of understanding her thoughts before she had them. How her brain had spun with the things they would do together. She'd give anything to know what he thinks of her collecting the medallion alone. She is certain Sol would wish her well.

Unclasping her handbag, she finds a tissue and balls it in her hand, readying herself in case she cries. She must remember, upstairs, to check that her husband brought his black socks for the ceremony. She must remember to find her good lipstick and put it into her purse. Mrs Yalow watches the girl slide her slender arms into her coat.

Lena is studying her curiously again, but this part Mrs Yalow will keep to herself.

Winning does not mean only joy will follow. Winning does not stop sadness. You have to be tougher than all that and forget the faceless men from your past who failed to have faith in you, who pointed out that you were indeed a woman, and not a good bet to join their program, their hospital, their team. To be obsessed with fairness, with what is owed, well, that mustn't enter into it. Not today. Certainly not tomorrow. Focus on all the luck you have received. Polish it like a coin.

CORN QUEEN

1983 | BARBARA McCLINTOCK | PHYSIOLOGY OR MEDICINE

Prize motivation: 'for her discovery of mobile genetic elements'

THE TOWN'S ANNUAL CORN PARADE runs on the first Saturday in August. When I was a kid, it was great. Best day of the year, everyone agreed. But it's been getting worse: fewer floats, dwindling popcorn flavours, healthier snacks. The year before last, the school marching band got banned because they were fooling around while they waited on Heron Street. When confronted by Mayor McBride, who fought his way through the trees at the back of the Ryans' property, the drummers and the trumpeters unlocked lips and picked up their hats from the bitumen where they'd thrown them down in ecstasy. The baton twirlers and the triangle players re-buttoned their shirts and put up a fight, saying they were on their own dime and could do as they damn well pleased. Mayor McBride broke at least three batons. So last year there was no marching band at all, just the music of Simon and Garfunkel coming from McBride's own stereo that he loaded onto the back of his son's pickup and slotted into the parade.

And then last year, protesters threatened to disrupt the parade, but they stayed well away – perhaps because of the Simon and Garfunkel. Kirk County corn has been GMO for a couple of years, and the hippies don't like it. Flyers began appearing in letterboxes across town, and citizens read the flyers because they were made to resemble editions of the agricultural magazine *Corn Alert!* (hippies being clever, who knew?). But instead of neatly typed, informative columns about physiological stalk lodging and push tests and stalk cannibalisation, they made gnarly claims about the effects of GMO corn on men's virility, and Roundup being detected in the bellies of pregnant mice. Most of our neighbours tore up the fake newsletters. The Schrobacks built a weedy little bonfire in their front yard. That shredded-up hippie paper took a long time to burn.

My fear about being Corn Queen and leading this year's Corn Parade is planted, like a seed, by Angie Hofmann. I hear her big, beaky voice while I'm walking through Market Park on my way home from school. 'No-one actually believes she'll go through with it, do they?' Angie says, perched on top of the jungle gym like a permed, lip-glossed prehistoric bird.

'Sure she will,' says Patty Horn, who does study period with me.

'It *used* to be good. Going downhill for years,' Angie says. 'That's why Connie won.'

'Connie Kruger is a grade-A choker,' chimes in Timothy Stead, who is pale and meaty and looks put together like a shish kebab. He's on the ground with his feet in the sand. His arms are above his head while he sways, leaning his huge body against the hot metal rungs.

I choked during the debate-team heats. I choked when I stood up to give my eighth-grade book report on *Sarah, Plain and Tall*. I choked on the penalty shoot-out in last year's final against Voigt Academy. That's what Timothy means. When I think about the

Corn Parade in two days' time, my stomach threshes, which I'm hoping will improve.

I don't think Angie, Patty and Timothy have spotted me on the sidewalk. It's a summer's day with the heat rising up off the Market Park pond. Some ducks and their babies are turning circles in the water.

When she was my age, my mother was crowned Corn Queen. Smiling, shining in old photos, her hands in long white gloves. I'd applied partly because it might make Dad happy, what with Mama and everything, but also in the hopes of winning the seventy-five-dollar prize. And I won. Not Patty. Not Angie. Surely I can lead the parade, sit with my shoulders back and a grin on my face, waving at all those sticky kids. Jake Bauer, the Chamber of Commerce president's son, is going to film the whole thing with a Video8 camcorder he's brought back from college. I'll be on tape forever.

The mother duck flicks her way out of the pond and yells at her babies to follow.

'Hey,' I decide to call out.

Angie says, 'Crap,' and wobbles up there, reaching out to hold on tight.

'Hi, Connie.' Patty drops to the ground with a thump. 'Excited for the parade?'

'I'm excited,' I tell Patty, as I glare at Timothy. 'I'm really fucking excited.'

Two days later and an hour to showtime, and I've thrown up twice. Dad and my twin brother, Raymond, find me sitting on the edge of the bathtub, my head in my hands. How did those marching-band kids do it? Not the fondling bit – but the bit where they could handle all those eyes on them. I picture myself on that throne, smiling out to the crowd, the pulse of waving flags, the hot sun dinging around in the sky and people calling out: *Connie! Connie! Wave to us!*

'I'm a choker,' I manage to say.

'You *were* a choker,' Raymond replies brightly. 'But not anymore.' He hands me a towel for my face.

Dad says, 'What's a choker?'

I should never have agreed to this. 'Give me a minute,' I say.

I close the bathroom door and stand in front of the mirror. I practised my eyeliner last week, but now it's a sooty mess. The lemon dress is floppy across my shoulders.

I come out to find Raymond, his knees tucked to his chest, on the floor against the kitchen counter and Dad sitting at the table, his hands folded together. I know Dad will wait for me to speak first.

Eventually I say, 'Dad, no. Please. I can't be Corn Queen.'

Dad, well, he is crestfallen. I wish I were a different girl, one who is calm and confident and who thinks dressing up in her dead mother's silk bridesmaid dress with a papier-mâché kernel-shaped bonnet is her idea of fun. And one day I might be. But not today, not this year.

'I'm sorry, Dad.' I'm prone to crying in front of my father and I feel it coming on here. Predictable. If I don't want to be Corn Queen, what *do* I want? What hope is there for me, I wonder, beginning to wail.

'Okay, Connie,' he says. 'Okay, all right.' He gestures for me to come over. I sit on his lap and put my little hand into his big hand. Dad does a huge sigh. 'Nobody wants to see a sad Corn Queen, do they?'

'But the parade is in an hour.' I grip the skirt of my mother's beautiful old dress. 'Oh, god. I can't do it, I can't do it.'

A tiny voice pipes up: 'I'll do it.'

Raymond.

'You'll do what?' Dad asks.

Raymond clears his throat then says something amazing. 'I'll be Corn Queen. So Connie doesn't have to.'

I shouldn't think of him as my baby brother since technically he's only two minutes younger than me, but there's something so humble and sweet about him. He and I look similar, but no boy has ever been Corn Queen. Last week I caught him rifling through Mama's wardrobe. My brain clicks a little. 'You?' I say.

'Corn Queen?' Dad says.

Raymond nods and sort of slinks out and comes over. He can't seem to find any words. Like the time after our mother died when he cut out individual letters from an edition of *Corn Alert!* and arranged them across Dad's mirror to spell out how he was feeling.

I turn to Dad, not knowing in the slightest how he will take this. Dad, who keeps a collection of over one hundred antique bear traps and who once ate a cigarette to show me how bad smoking is. Most boys in Haines play football, poke at dead things on the road, circle girls on their bikes in the parking lot of the Super Buy. But Raymond isn't most boys.

I hear the kitchen clock and the sound of the sprinkler *chock-chocking* across the front lawn. In less than an hour, one of us has to be on that float. I put a sweaty hand on Dad's arm. My heart is racing again: what will people like Angie and Patty and Timothy say? Raymond is gentler than I am and would never defend himself by screaming out curse words across Market Park. Maybe I can rally. Find my courage. I try to picture myself on the float, everyone watching, but my brain shoots away from the idea like a squid releasing ink. Dad and I search each other's eyes till, finally, I shake my head slowly.

Dad claps a hand on Raymond's shoulder. 'You sure you want to help out your sister? Dress up on that float and what-not?'

'I can do that,' he says.

I've taken off the crown and set it on the table. Already my head and neck feel lighter.

Dad goes, 'I guess a Kruger family Corn Queen is better than no Corn Queen.'

Raymond's face lights up.

Parade officials stand around with their hands behind their backs, puffed up with importance. They wear straw boater hats and polo shirts tucked into their blue jeans. Our designated Corn Parade official is Bev Kessler, who's been chaperoning the Corn Queen float for approximately fifty years. She keeps antacids and Red Vines in her fanny pack, which she offers to Raymond to settle any nerves he might have, even though we told her it was *me* who had the nerves, and there aren't enough Red Vines in the world to make me want to trade places. I'm overcome with relief, seeing my other half up there. Raymond's wearing my heels. I'm back in my tennis shoes, bouncing on the hot bitumen.

I see my twin brother for all he is and for all he might be. He and I are no angiosperms, but we shared our mother's womb and popped right on out of her. We loved her from the inside, and our whole existence, even after she's gone, is a reflection of her.

Raymond shifts the folds of the dress around his legs. He raises both hands to touch the kernel bonnet again, but stops halfway, as if he's thinking, *Actually, it is perfect. Do not touch it.* The queen's float is run on propane, the top of it decorated in four hundred yellow chrysanthemums, two hundred gladioli, and three hundred and fifty blue bachelor buttons. A sign along the side shouts in giant letters: *Everything's comin' up corn!* The parade won't start for eight more minutes, but Raymond begins waving anyway. The sparrows in the trees – if there are sparrows in the trees – he's waving at them. Tilting and swivelling his hand like he's describing a peach to someone.

I run a hand gently over a swathe of bachelor buttons. I hope he knows how wonderful he looks. Tina Yared wore a yellow dress with a matching bolero to prom two years ago, but that was nothing compared to my radiant twin brother.

On the corner of South and Lockwood, Timothy Stead and his grubby little brothers sit in the kerb, swiping their tennis racquets through the air, totally bored. Timothy Stead is just dirty that he didn't make the cut to press play on Mayor McBride's stereo system this year. Rumour has it Simon and Garfunkel are out; The Eagles are in.

'I'll be watching you the whole way,' I tell Raymond.

Bev keeps checking her watch. I'm itching for her to give us the nod.

'Raymond,' Bev says, 'the future is just around that bend.' She points along the parade route. First it goes under Duckworth Bridge which, despite everyone's best efforts, means at least one float per year gets crushed and all its inhabitants scatter like a school of fish. Once, someone suggested the parade should start beyond the bridge so as to avoid the risk of decapitation. But that man was new to Haines, and didn't understand tradition, and we never saw him again.

Bev hasn't finished. 'Today is yours for the *taking!*'

'Thanks, Bev,' Raymond calls out.

'Thank *you*, Corn Queen,' Bev says. She salutes my brother, then slips me another Red Vine.

Ahead of us, Rory Bisker buffs the curvaceous engine of his dark green tractor. Like everything else, Rory's family's tractor is a tradition in Haines. Corn Queen gets the first float, but the Bisker family tractor puttering to the top of Main Street signals to all Hainesians that the queen is coming. Imagine their faces when they spot Raymond, when they go find my father in the crowd to shake his hand.

And then I hear drums. A trumpet puncturing the air. Heavy footfalls coming from beyond Duckworth Bridge, where the citizens of Haines have lined Main Street to sit in folding chairs and hoist children up for a better view. There'll be flags and ice cream and popcorn in blue-and-white paper cups. Raymond is wide-eyed. It sounds like a marching band, which can't be right. There's no marching band this year; all those horny teenagers are boycotting the parade and staying home to give one another hickeys in peace.

A dozen people dressed in neon-green coveralls are heading towards us, up the rise of South Street.

I look at Bev. 'What's going on?'

'Who are they?' she yells back at me. Then in their direction she barks, 'Who are you?'

They're chanting something. I wonder if this is just a different way of signalling that it's time for Raymond and his propane-powered float to get moving, to wake up from its idling state and shake its great floral coat in the sun. Maybe the walkie-talkies have failed.

Thinking of our mother's face, I'm about ready to cry again.

Little things: she used to park the car on the driveway and turn to the two of us in the back seat, blowing kisses. Then before we went inside, she'd move the mirror to fix her hair, but she moved it so she could see us in the back while she beamed, pins in her mouth, her eyes dancing between us.

'Go!' I yell out to my brother.

'Go?'

'Yes!'

'You sure?'

Then one of the green people lifts a megaphone to their face and a tinny voice yells, 'Stop Haines corn! No GMO! Stop Haines corn! No GMO!'

Bev says, 'Oh, *shit.*' She zips up her fanny pack and starts running for them.

GROWTH

1986 | RITA LEVI-MONTALCINI | PHYSIOLOGY OR MEDICINE

Prize motivation: 'for their discoveries of growth factors'

'YOU'RE HAVING SECOND THOUGHTS, AREN'T YOU?' Estelle, my PhD supervisor, asks me. 'Wait. Don't answer that. Don't think you're the first.'

'I know that. And I'm not having second thoughts.'

We're in her office, late one Friday. I've given my final tutorial for the semester. Those third-years who always sit up the front of my classroom baked brownies for everyone. The jacarandas are out. Exams are coming up.

'You are something like *six weeks* from the next milestone,' Estelle says.

'I know,' I say. 'Six weeks.'

'Six.'

'But what difference does it make?'

'Does *what* make?' Estelle asks.

'What's the point in all this?' I motion to her desk, where I've delivered my most recent stack of thesis pages, loose-leaf, like she prefers. 'It's not *important*,' I say.

Estelle has her hands on her hips. She stares at me. 'Terrible waste of time,' she finally says.

'I'm serious.'

'Badly written.'

'Estelle. I'm very self-conscious about producing ninety thousand words on representations of play in mid-twentieth-century children's literature through the lens of object-oriented ontology.'

'This is great timing,' she says. From her hips she flashes me a pair of thumbs up.

'You know I'm good at timing,' I say. 'But how about staying alive? Or researching something that's useful and life-changing? With everything going on in the world.'

'You writing or not writing this is not going to change the world. I'm sorry.'

'It's all pointless.'

'Take the weekend off,' Estelle says. 'I insist.'

'You're the one who told me about the documentary,' I say.

In the documentary you see Rita in old age living with her twin sister, Paola, an artist, in an apartment in Rome filled with plants and Paola's canvases stacked against the walls. Rita was still travelling the world, though not as much, giving talks and interviews about nerve growth factor and what happens when you educate girls – all girls – properly. Rita and Paola are bird-like, tiny women, always touching each other on the wrists and not needing to speak in full sentences, leaning in close, gold bracelets chiming.

When they were young, they played with their mother's jewellery. They looped necklaces up their arms and poked their fingers into rings. They gave themselves high voices so no-one would notice they hadn't grown up yet. Why all these many moments of bliss when we're so young and unable to remember them later in life? I came up with a theory about the brain – that forgetting our youthful joy is the brain's way of protecting us from future sadness and a life that can never live up to that initial bliss – and Estelle put up her hand and said, 'I'm gonna stop you right there.' Because neurology has absolutely zero to do with what I'm studying, a first draft of which is due in less than six weeks, and she is doing her best to keep me on track. But Estelle always listens – maybe stands to go water the fern on her office windowsill – when I bring up my father in the context of my research.

'Don't go down that rabbit hole,' Estelle says, regarding me with her violet eyes. She is tall with cropped blonde hair. She has two grown-up daughters and is fluent in four languages. 'But you already have, haven't you?'

When I get home I ring the hospital. He had a good day, they tell me. Ate dinner. Had a chat. Nothing to report.

I try to fall asleep at about 10 pm but that only lasts a minute. I turn the light back on and pick up the book on Rita.

She was around for World War I, World War II, the Vietnam War and all the things in between. Reminds me of that Greenland shark scientists found that's been gliding around since Shakespeare. Reminds me of those ancient, deep-sea giant tube worms that weren't even discovered till 1977. Reminds me of programmed cell death, which is also in the documentary. Reminds me that when cells do not commit cell suicide in the way they're supposed to, a person might become sick. And if cells die *too* much, a person becomes sick then as well.

Hitler and Mussolini were out to get Rita. Men with that much power, set on destroying her. If not her personally, then her kind generally – but who's to say that what happened back then wasn't *absolutely* personal? Estelle is good at reminding me that so many things I think aren't personal (the way my father's family have abrogated all responsibility for him and won't call me on the phone; the fact that I wasn't paid for that work I did for Professor Bruno) actually are. And all the things we assume are personal – like the red traffic light when we're late for class or the cafe running out of eggs just as we get there – have absolutely nothing to do with us.

Rita was one hundred and three when she died. Didn't care for sleep. Those people who talk about getting by on so little: are they getting more sleep than they say they are or are they actually surviving on even *less*? She ate modestly. Another rabbit hole. Loads of evidence nowadays about what intermittent fasting can do for you. More energy. Luminous skin. Loss of belly fat. Some reports that it even changes the expression of your genes. Thicker hair. We humans were never meant to eat a family-sized bowl of carbonara for dinner, lying on our backs on a too-short couch, at half past eight, changing the font on our thesis back and forth. We were never meant to consume four rows of chocolate, then drink a scorching cup of tea to make amends. Brush our teeth. Go straight to bed.

And she didn't merely fast and get by on a few hours of rest. Each day, Rita dropped nerve growth factor straight into her eyeballs, the body able to absorb it immediately through the cornea. She said it kept her young.

Not being employable at her university, not being safe, barely being visible, having to convince her father that *no*, she did not want to be a wife and mother, that *yes*, he should trust her enough with her vision for her future. That not being a wife and mother – it wouldn't become something she'd regret later in life. What a thing for a father to say and do. What a thing to have to convince him of.

And beyond not being employable, she and her family were being hunted. British bombs, then American, then German. Getting a note, or a phone call perhaps, to say you couldn't keep your job at the university until finally she thought it was safer for everyone if she simply left.

So she had this idea and she cycled the countryside asking for hen eggs from her neighbours. Did she pay for them? Convince them she needed eggs to feed children she did not have? Was she as good at haggling as my father once was? Till, in the end, those farmers were handing over baskets of eggs and they were farewelling the back of a spindly girl on a bicycle shooting down the hill, going: *Wait a second. Aren't we in a war? Why am I giving my chickens away?*

Back home, where other girls her age would have set themselves up to do needlepoint beside a windowpane or compose a poem about the leaves on the trees in Turin turning apple-red, she made a laboratory in her bedroom, wanting to know if you manipulate this part of the chick embryo what effect does it have on this other part? And there were other labs, in other bedrooms in the countryside, one in a basement in Florence. Getting pursued, being afraid, but perhaps also getting *fed up*. Having to, yet again, tuck that microscope and those slides under her wing. Grabbing a suitcase at night, wondering about the limbs of those chicks in her eggs. All the while running. Reminds me of my song and dance when I spilt water over my laptop, the *hurdle* that seemed to represent. The angry emails I shot off to Estelle, saying I'd be late with my chapter. Not her fault, I added. But also not *not* her fault, I didn't say.

Reminds me of universities cutting funding. Reminds me of governments wanting more from universities with less. Reminds me of the time Estelle told me that her creative work – her gorgeous novels – will no longer count towards her ranking and chances for promotion. Even though she's a creative writing professor. Even though she's won loads of awards and people – regular people, not just academics – know her by name and sometimes even by sight. Our head of school told her to stop bothering, or to do it in her own time. Of course it was up to Estelle what she did for fun.

Estelle told me all this, laughing, one afternoon when we walked to get coffee across the wide green lawn – this was before jacaranda season – and down past the campus childcare centre and one of the gyms. How could she laugh about it? I was horrified. But she's been in this game long enough to ride the waves, to wait to see precisely which beach she gets spat up on. As we neared the cafe, she sidestepped some dog shit. She paid for my coffee.

'Take the weekend off,' she reminds me in an email that I see on my phone right before midnight on Friday. Reminds me of the time I started a sleep-detox routine to get me through my master's. It meant no phone in the bedroom at night, no TV after eight o'clock. Kitchens are places for eating; bedrooms are places for sleeping. Teach your brain to recognise good habits. But at midnight I'm still up and I see her email.

I wake up late on Saturday morning and have to rush around. I go visit Dad at the hospital. I've brought him random things from home that I could fit into the basket of my bike. He loves the blueberries, and the smoothie still cold in its KeepCup. He points into my bag and says he loves the *idea* of the pretzels.

'I'm a crap daughter,' I say, wanting to be reassured.

'No, no,' he says. 'Come here, come here.' He kisses me on the forehead.

I see the pair of them, Rita and Paola, bent towards each other in youth and beyond, so connected and loving. I see them being hunted by those tyrants, from place to place. Did Paola use the eggs Rita gathered, too, in some way? Did she grind up the shells and press them into her paintings? They cared for each other and fed each other. Both outlived those terrible men.

WITNESSING

1988 | GERTRUDE B. ELION | PHYSIOLOGY OR MEDICINE

Prize motivation: 'for their discoveries of
important principles for drug treatment'

LATE ONE SATURDAY MORNING, EMMA sat at the kitchen table with her mother and her aunty, eating cake. They were discussing ways that Emma's mother, Libby, might choose to die. Libby had cancer. It had started in her stomach but now it was everywhere. It had a mind of its own.

Emma dragged her index finger up the side of the cake, which she and Aunty Josie had made from lemons their neighbour had placed in a wire basket and left on their front step. Emma rubbed her index finger against her thumb, tacking the thick white icing together then apart then together again.

'Let me try that,' Libby said, scooping up a globule from a piece of cake that wasn't even hers. 'Delicious,' she said. 'Next time let's make a cake out of icing and the icing out of the cake.'

Emma thought her mother was trying to change the subject, and she was glad. It was about eleven o'clock and they had eaten their breakfast at the table, the sun shining on their white plates. Someone, most likely Aunty Josie since she wasn't used to living the way Libby and Emma lived, had cleared their dishes into the sink. But no-one had really left the kitchen. Libby had gone for a wee. Emma had dug out a toothpick from a box on the kitchen bench and worked a piece of spinach out from her teeth. Now, the toothpick lay in spitty splinters beside her water glass. Breakfast had become morning tea. Aunty Josie had filled the kettle and washed all the mugs in the house before dropping teabags into three of them. Libby and Emma sat sighing. Occasionally Libby leaned in and Emma kissed her. Now their cheeks were covered in the lemon icing.

'I want you to know,' Libby said, pointing at her daughter, 'that the world is not a dangerous place.'

'Okay, sure,' Emma said.

Aunty Josie said, 'What about those trucks driving into crowds of people?' She'd taken the cutlery out of its drawer and she rested against the sink, rubbing each piece of silverware vigorously.

They'd all seen footage like that. In the aftermath, victims' objects strewn across empty streets. Shoes and hats, sunglasses – now broken.

Libby yawned. 'Emma, you see any loonies in a van coming for you? You run. Promise me.'

Libby had opted out of more chemotherapy. She said she didn't see the point, hated how it made her feel. She told a joke about it: *Oh, you don't like how it makes you feel? There's a support group for that. It's called 'everybody' and they meet at the bar.*

The neighbour who'd dropped off the lemons in the wire basket came and knocked on their door. 'Don't worry about returning the basket,' she said, peering around Emma into the hall behind her.

'Okay,' Emma replied.

'If you did want to leave it out on your verandah, though, it would save you having to drop it back.'

'So you do want it back?'

'Actually,' their neighbour said, 'don't even worry about it. In fact, you keep it, you and your mum.'

'Do you like lemons?' Emma asked.

'I love them,' their neighbour said. 'Some people think they have healing properties.'

'We definitely believe that,' Emma said, shutting the door with a wave.

Half an hour later there was another knock. Emma went straight to the front door and opened it. Two boys stood there, one on the verandah and the other on the top step. Both wore white button-down shirts with ties.

It took Emma half a second to speak. 'Mark.'

'Emma.'

'Why are you at my house?'

Mark opened his mouth, then closed it again. 'This is Shaun,' Mark finally said. 'Shaun, this is Emma.'

'Hi. Mark and I go to school together. That's why this is weird.'

Mark cleared his throat. 'I'm not embarrassed to be here.'

'I didn't say you *should* be. I'm just saying it's weird.'

'We're witnessing in your neighbourhood. I didn't know you lived here.'

Mark and Emma used to live near each other – before her parents' divorce. When they were kids, they played together in Mark's bedroom. Test Match was set up in one corner, its bowler preparing to heave that tiny red ball that looked precisely like a Jaffa. Mark's bed was pushed up against the wall. One Easter, Emma presented Mark with a chocolate egg, cupped perfectly in her hands, and wrapped in blue foil. *Thank you for the chocolate,*

Mark said. *I love chocolate.* He told her he was a Jehovah's Witness and didn't want to say the words 'Easter egg'. He broke it in half with his teeth and shared it with her.

'Hey, I heard about your mum.'

Emma raised her eyebrows.

'I'm sorry. I hope she's okay.'

'My aunty is staying with us. She thinks we live like pigs, but she's a good cook, and Mum seems less fucking manic when she's here.'

On the top step, Shaun glanced away. There was a pink ring of acne around his chin. He touched it with his hand.

Emma looked up at the sky. It was a hard, clear summer's day. She slid a finger beneath the strap of her bra and fixed it in place. Maybe later she would go for a swim. She could probably convince her mother to come.

'Is this still your religion?' Emma asked. She heard Josie inside, the scrape of dining chairs on the tiles. Emma shut the door behind her. 'Is this what you do on a Saturday?'

'My dad's down there,' Mark said, pointing to a red station wagon on the street. The bag on Mark's shoulder had a long strap. He turned back and the bag swung with him. 'This is what I sometimes do on a Saturday.'

Emma thought of the neighbours in her street. Surely none of them answered the door when they saw these people in their shirts and ties coming. Poor Mark. Hours filled with other people's pity, their anger, their embarrassment.

'My dad thinks that God didn't intend for there to be death, for people to die. Cells are replaced over and over and over. Maybe we could one day live forever. Without suffering.'

'Maybe your dad is a bit clueless.'

Mark seemed to think it over. 'Maybe.' He tugged at his tie. Emma thought he might take it off. But instead he tightened it. The skin of his neck was pocked with tiny black dots, from shaving, Emma presumed.

Shaun had escaped down the steps. He was crouched on the front lawn, the fingers of one hand forked into the grass. His bag was on the ground next to his foot. Josie's car was parked metres away.

'It would be good, though, wouldn't it? Your mum getting better?'

Emma knew Libby wasn't going to make it to the end of the year. Instead, Josie would look after her, help her finish her last year of high school. After that, Emma could do what she liked. Josie and Patrick would be a phone call away in Gladstone. Libby did not hide the emails from Exit International. On nights Emma stood outside her mother's room, drinking milk from a glass, she listened for her breathing. She'd touch her forehead to the door. *Bed down*, Libby would call out. *I'm in bed*, Emma would reply.

Emma pointed. 'What's in your bag?'

'Literature for you to read,' Mark said. 'It's free, if you want it.'

He didn't hand it over, but held up a pamphlet. On its cover: two faces, one in the bottom left corner and one in the bottom right. Above them the sky was muscular and whipped blue: a dark and heavy storm.

'You don't actually believe this stuff, do you?' Emma asked. 'I mean, sorry.'

Mark said, 'Yes.' He gave a small smile. 'Why else would I be here?'

Emma came into the kitchen, sat at the table where the cake had been cleared away, and explained to Josie about Mark turning up at the house, how they had once been best friends – ages ago, anyway – and how completely awkward it had been seeing him on her verandah. For years they'd barely noticed each other at high school.

'Isn't it messed up how people change?' she asked Josie. 'Isn't it creepy how people have these secret lives?'

'Don't get angry at me, blossom.'

'I'm not. I just feel weird about it and I wish he hadn't come to my house.'

'You can still be his friend.'

'No, I can't.'

'Look, you don't want to get to my age and think that you should have been nicer to someone.'

'I won't mind.'

'Yes,' Josie said. 'You will.'

'I'm nice.'

'There's nice and then there's nice. Once, your grandfather found out there was a woman living in the car park beneath his office. Had a sleeping bag, and a garbage bag with shoes and food and things in it. Instead of calling the police or the building manager or whatever, he organised for the cafe down the road to deliver her lunch every day. She was there for months.'

'You're right. I could never be that nice.'

'You don't have to be like Grandad Bill. Just ... make someone else feel good even if you don't want to.'

'That sounds rapey.'

'Oh, for god's *sake*, Emma,' Josie said, and gathered the three mugs together with a clunk and walked out. But she returned a minute later, with the mugs, because where else would she put them? And she touched Emma on the arm. 'Forget I said anything.'

'No. I thought about what you said and you're right. It was good what you said.'

'Oh, Emma.'

They started playing on their phones, sitting together at the table. Josie typed out a text. She had a boyfriend, Patrick, in Gladstone. He had short greasy hair and small meaty hands and a young son named Isaac. Patrick drove a twin cab with a toddler seat strapped in the back. He had once lost his son in the bathrooms of a Bunnings for more than forty-five minutes. Apparently Patrick's ex-wife was extremely good-natured about the whole thing, Josie assured them, about their being together and Josie becoming Isaac's sort-of mother. It made it easier on them all. When Emma asked Patrick what he had gone to Bunnings to buy, he remembered precisely. Patrick said he thought they might give him the things for free, his son having got lost in their bathrooms, but they didn't. Emma thought he was a bit dim, but her aunty had always liked being smarter than everyone else.

Libby came back from bringing in the laundry. She sat down slowly and brought a washcloth to her face. 'I could smother myself,' she said. 'That's one way.'

'You could never,' Josie said. She had her blue diary open in front of her. She was crossing something out. 'It isn't possible.'

'Is it like tickling, then?' Emma moved to her mother's side. 'The way you can't tickle yourself?'

At the word *tickle*, Libby drew her right hand up and down her left arm, slowly and lovingly. She closed her eyes. Emma and Josie watched her. Then Libby opened her eyes and leaned in to Emma for a nose rub. They stayed like that, face to face, for a long time.

Josie thought they looked so much alike. Emma was a freshly drawn version of her mother. Emma's bra strap fell down her bare shoulder. Josie wanted to slip it back up. Nothing in Libby and Emma's house fitted properly or was clean or tidy or sharp or shiny or matching or new. The cake platter had belonged to her and Libby's grandmother. It was the nicest thing in this house, Josie thought, knowing that was an exaggeration. Josie could hardly stand to be here, but it was important she try. She couldn't wait to get back to Patrick. He would make her spaghetti and meatballs. The house would smell of vanilla. The kitchen benches would be sponged down, and her underwear would be clean and sunny and folded on their bed.

Emma kissed her mother goodnight, watching her settle back on the pillows. Asleep within seconds.

A flurry of sadness went through her. Emma thought of all the things her mother would miss. Saw herself waving goodbye at an airport departure gate. She pictured herself years from now finding one of Libby's earrings buried in a handbag. She remembered Christmas nut roasts they laboured over for hours only to throw away, devouring wax-papered after-dinner mints instead, laughing at how terribly they cooked vegetarian food. Emma had been a difficult child, not playing well with others and wailing when her mother tried to drop her at child care, tried to unpeel her limbs from her body and pass her to the teacher. So Libby gave in and set up a day care at home for Emma and a few other local kids, whose parents paid her, the type of laid-back parents who loved that Libby would open her fridge and feed their children whatever food was inside.

She and Libby shared secrets, always. Even now Emma can recall the loving chamber of that time. When Emma's dad, David, gently suggested something *other than a nut roast* for Christmas dinner, they obliged him politely, as though he were a shop assistant who wouldn't leave them alone. Pitying him, they passed him the box of mints to eat.

~

Josie was by her sister's side when Libby died three months later, more or less on schedule. Libby was not one to follow rules or timetables, but Josie saw it more like Libby wanting no fuss, wanting to show her daughter that life tilted towards death, then back to life quickly. But this was absurd, Josie knew. There was a total absence of will and motivation in the exact moment a person's body irretrievably changed temperature, setting the organs on a course towards rot. On the phone with her grandparents, Emma used the words *lost her battle*, but those words made Josie sick, although she didn't say so.

That whole year when Libby had talked and half-joked about suicide now seemed ghoulish. Instead, she had been transferred to a hospice, and she died there naturally.

At the funeral home, after the service, a middle-aged staffer in navy heels and black stockings sought out Josie to offer a muffin on a paper napkin and a cup of tea. David came and made himself useful, carrying around the damn guest book the funeral home had supplied. Watching him cuddle Emma and be bailed up for a long conversation about termites with a pest-controller uncle, Josie thought how lucky her sister had been to have a husband who was good, even though it didn't work out. Libby and Josie's former high-school principal came. So did the loved-up young couple who'd bought Libby and David's house after the divorce. One of Libby's old boyfriends appeared in a beautiful suit and tie, but left without speaking to anyone. Children on her mother's side – Josie's second cousins – mushed a bowl of strawberries into a corner of the carpet, and the woman in the navy shoes dabbed at it with more napkins, telling the children it was okay, that no-one would get into trouble. That was the high point. Even with her parents stoic and loving beside her, Josie felt orphaned.

She watched Emma sit with the girlfriends she'd invited from school. None of them ate anything, and they played on their phones then held hands when they followed Emma to the bathroom. Emma avoided Josie till that night when she called out for Josie to lie with her in her double bed, and she stayed awake while Emma cried beside her. The boy Mark visited as well and, for a week or so after, Emma curled up on the sofa at night with an old Bible from their bookshelf. Then Josie found it back in its place on the shelf, and they never spoke about it.

Emma finished school. For one night the house was alive with teenagers who came round for a party. Josie was amused by their good manners. She lay, ankles crossed, propped up on cushions in the guest room, with the door shut, reading half a page of some book every now and then but mostly staring at the wall and recalling parties from her own youth – the breakages, the pot, the sex in the neighbours' front yard. Instead, Emma's friends sat around a laptop, drinking and playing music through modest portable speakers. When Josie went into the kitchen, one of them offered to make her a coffee. In the morning the floor was swept, the bottles were upright in the recycling bin, and the dishes rinsed and stacked. While Emma slept off her hangover, Josie brought in their washing. Her feet boiled on the concrete. In the air was the smell of Christmas. The cicadas were silent during the day.

In mid-January, Emma decided to accompany Josie back to Gladstone. She deferred her university course, saying she would not go, probably ever, and maybe she would find something to do in North Queensland. Josie had been travelling back and forth from Brisbane to Gladstone for months. Patrick would welcome them both. Isaac, on the weekends he was with his father, would love having Emma around.

They organised Libby and Emma's house. Three of Emma's friends would live there for a bit, excited to be out of home for their first year of university. They sat together at the kitchen table – eyes concentrating on the few bits of paper Josie had drawn up, exquisitely polite, chins in hands, one girl with a hickey like a pressed thumb against her neck – listening to Josie put in place an arrangement for six months, just to see how everything went. Could Josie bring herself to tell the girl with the hickey that there were fewer years between the two of them than the teenager probably suspected? Eighteen? Nineteen? But Josie stopped herself. She explained the bank account set up for rent deposits, which would work well enough until any of them knew how permanent this all was. Emma cooked pizzas for everyone and she ate her piece messily at the table. She dragged her fingers through the tomato sauce.

While they were cleaning out the house in the summer heat, Josie spied a dead snake beside the patio, painfully bloated. She found a shoebox of postcards her sister had received from David when he was teaching English in Kyoto. The sun clanged in the sky. Josie came out with the box of letters to show Emma, and saw the snake once more – should have dealt with it the first time – and vomited.

The car was packed up. Josie let Emma drive the first hour out of Brisbane. She had her Ls but was months off her Ps and needed to make up about forty hours before her driving test. Emma was a good driver, better than Josie had been at her age.

'Let's stop here.' Josie pointed to a BP up ahead off the highway. It had a wide, flat roof over dozens of petrol bowsers. In the car park, Emma pulled expertly into a tight spot.

Inside, Josie watched her niece head off to the bathrooms. She looked so alone: really, truly isolated. A twisted, messy plait swung almost down to her bottom. There were flecks of mud on the backs of her legs, and she was barefoot on the cold tiles. Josie felt a wave of despair. What work would she do and who would she meet? Nothing good had ever come of moving somewhere because it was the lesser of two evils.

In a minute Emma was back, shaking water from her hands, coming towards her and the cabinet of pastries and muffins.

'Can I get a piece of cake?' she asked.

'You can have whatever you want, blossom,' Josie said.

Together they joined the cafe queue. Josie touched her niece's elbow. Emma didn't love hugs, so these touches – dozens of them all day – could add up to something.

When they got to the front of the line, Emma pointed to a slice of cake, thick with pale icing, and Josie paid. Emma took the white plate and ran her thumbnail around the icing. She snatched two forks out of a basket and made a beeline for a table and chairs. The coffee machines were spitting steam. A barista whacked against a knock bin. Josie watched Emma take the first few bites and then push the plate away.

'Eight bucks. Sorry, Josie.'

'It's all right.'

'That's disgusting. Don't eat it.'

'Okay,' Josie said, 'I won't.'

Emma toyed with her fork then let it clatter onto the tabletop. Josie couldn't take her eyes off her. She was looking more and more like Libby every day, and Josie was stricken with the knowledge that she would be around to see the resemblance grow in the years to come, like a pair of lines converging. She couldn't allow Emma to see her cry. Josie knew her sister wouldn't return and so she needed to put that grief somewhere, needed to chase it out.

She stood up. 'Back in a sec.'

Emma held up her hand for Josie to stay. 'Wait. Do you think Patrick will be okay having me around? And Isaac?'

'Oh, they're going to *love* it.'

Emma laid her hands flat on the table and stared at them. 'And do you think I'm going to drive you nuts?'

'No. Listen, hon.' Josie stepped closer. 'The boys will be waiting for you. They'll have balloons, they'll have cake, they'll have a room made up for you. They'll be waiting for us both.'

FRUIT FLIES

1995 | CHRISTIANE NÜSSLEIN-VOLHARD | PHYSIOLOGY OR MEDICINE

Prize motivation: 'for their discoveries concerning the genetic control of early embryonic development'

AFTERWARDS, A COUNSELLOR CAME TO SCHOOL to follow us around. Her name was Klara. Our headmaster introduced her to our grade at assembly and told us why she was here, then at lunch she zeroed in on our table and plonked herself down, right next to me. I thought about messing with her, saying that I'd once strung Max along for months, pretending I was into him till I finally told him he was a loser, a weirdo, not worth my time. I thought about feeding all that to her, just because something like this hadn't happened before. But I said, 'I guess I knew him. He lent me some spinach for a recipe I did.'

'Sorry? Spinach?' Klara said.

'Like, we had to bring our ingredients for home ec. It was a veggie slice or something, and if you didn't bring all your ingredients you couldn't cook and you had to sit at a desk and write. He saw I was pissed off that I'd forgotten the spinach and so he gave me half of his. Said his mum bought him a huge bunch. I remember that. He said, *She wants me to learn how to cook.*'

'When was this?'

'Ages ago. Grade eight, I guess.'

My boyfriend, Nick, leaned across the picnic table and clarified things for this woman. 'Bridie's not saying she and Max were best friends.'

I nodded at Klara. 'Yeah. I'm not saying I *knew* him,' I said. 'I dunno. That's just what I remember.'

Our school was running an art prize for the first time. My teacher, Mrs Eames, had recently come over from St Ita's and kept going on about how they offered a cash award each year and organised a show. The idea was to hang paintings on the library walls, push desks together and sit the sculptures on top. Wine and nuts and whatever for all the parents she was sure would come. She was trying hard to make us excited. I didn't usually have it in me to match people's excitement, but I guess I felt sorry for her. She probably wished she was still at St Ita's. God knows what she'd done to get us instead.

'Go back to St Ita's, then,' Nick said, I guess to her, but through me, while we walked home one afternoon from school past the big storage garage. Kids made up stories about what people kept in there: dead bodies and apocalyptic amounts of porn, things like that. Someone's brother worked there one summer, and he always made jokes about having to air the place out when it got too humid, and the freaky shit he got to poke through. But for his story to work, you'd have to believe they handed out garage keys to any old teenager to look through people's private business.

'She's only trying to make things interesting,' I said. I found that I did this often, with Nick, changed my tune. He brought out something bitchy in me.

'You should enter,' Nick said, surprising me. He dug into his backpack and took out two cigarettes, then his lighter from his pocket. He lit mine first. Gestures like this were high on my mother's wishlist for my sisters and me. Not necessarily the cigarette part, but having a boyfriend do nice things for you, in a way that others might see. That was important.

I had a week left till the deadline. 'Maybe I will,' I said, agreeing with him for once. 'Maybe I'll ask Richie when we get to yours, see if he has any inspiration.'

Nick, scoffing, reached for my hand. 'As if he knows what's going on,' he said.

I watched Nick flick the end of his cigarette away from my leg. We stood at an intersection a few blocks from his house, waiting for the cars to pass. I pulled my hand away from his and got out my phone to start googling ideas for Mrs Eames's class. 'You shouldn't talk about your brother like that,' I said.

'Why not?' He looked the other way, into the traffic.

'It's mean. It's cruel.'

'Excuse me, I can talk about my family how I like. Richie knows he's slow.'

I hopped off the kerb. 'You just feel lucky it isn't you.' I was a step ahead.

'Pardon?' he said.

My heart quickened. I stared at my phone and kept walking. Once, I had called Max a horrible name. Klara the counsellor left before I could tell her that.

'You're always guilty because you're grateful you're not like Richie.'

'I don't like it when you speak that way,' Nick said, softening, when we got safely to the other side. 'You're not that person. Don't be so tough.' He brought his hand up to my hair. He rubbed my back between my shoulder blades.

Later that night, after Nick was asleep, I crawled out of his bed and went across the hallway to his brother's room. I didn't go in or anything. I held my hand against the door like they do in the movies. In the end I was surprised how nice that felt, how much I convinced myself I could sense Richie and understand him through the membrane of my palm. Their mother was talking on the phone in the kitchen downstairs. She never slept. Right at the beginning, when Nick and I started going out, I mentioned that I heard her long fingernails tapping on the countertop early one morning – I was just making conversation – and she went red and apologised all through breakfast. She loved having me over. It made Nick embarrassed how much she loved it.

I went to the bathroom, peed so I wouldn't get a UTI, sponged between my legs with a washer, which I tossed into the boys' laundry basket. Then I returned to Nick and tried to snuggle up against his back. But he moved and left me on the other side of the bed, feeling stranded.

I was wilful about Nick and him telling me what to do and say. The next night, at a party Nick didn't want to go to, I met James. He was twenty-nine and I could tell he liked me straight away. It didn't take long: we spoke for about an hour. James was a paramedic, he was new to town, recently back from a trip to Thailand, and so on. I got us both drinks, then we walked to the corner and went through some stranger's fence so we were in their yard, hidden by bushes. I felt his hands in my hair and around my back, under my shirt. James was very used to all this. None of it took him by surprise, just in case I thought for a moment that I was special. He wanted to fuck but in the end I told him no and he was pretty good about it, considering. On the way back to the party

I noticed orange peel in the gutter and a baby's nappy, wrapped up tight, pale like a ball of dough.

I'd seen the artist's work where he built a big glass box then put a dish of sugar and water in with some flies. Above them he hung a bug zapper. He called it *A Thousand Years*. I liked that title, because of how it sounded, but who knows why he called it that. Did he think the flies – even with the zapper – would last that long in there? Or, without the zapper, they'd survive on and on and on? Did he love the idea of people wondering about the title, and being confused by it, something a weirdo would want? Whatever the case, I avoided Nick and worked on my project all week. I called it *Forty-five Minutes*, which is the length of a single art period at our school.

After class I got Mrs Eames to stay back so I could show her my piece before the prize night. I'd made my version in an old fish tank the size of a shoebox. She touched it with her elegant hands while I looked down at my chewed-up fingernails. I pressed a bloodied finger to my lips and sucked it.

She stepped towards me. 'You look just like your sisters,' Mrs Eames said, 'but you're nothing like them, are you?'

Mrs Eames knew what I had done, knew I'd copied that man's work.

'I don't know,' I said. I felt myself about to cry. My sister Yvonne wouldn't have done to Nick what I did. Neither would my sister Charlotte. Temptations like that – if they did feel them, they would never act on them. My mother wouldn't have done what I did. She had a knack for caring for children and animals, in a quiet way, no fanfare. Anyone else would think she wasn't as smart as other people, as clever as my sisters and me, but it takes a lot to be that nice and make people around you feel good, always.

'Fine,' Mrs Eames said. 'Want to explain your piece to me?'

'Fruit flies are fascinating,' I said. I'd stopped myself from crying. I stared around at the aprons, on their hooks, spattered with paint. And the coils of wire, and the slabs of clay wrapped in plastic.

'In what way?'

'They multiply at rates that are interesting for scientists who research evolution.'

'And this is all your own work? Your own ideas?' She rested against the whiteboard, studying me.

I waited. Then I shook my head slowly. Mrs Eames began to nod. For a bit I was shaking my head at the same time as she was nodding.

Max's house was on stilts. I reached the verandah up a single set of stairs that led straight from the barrel-shaped letterbox at the footpath. The front of the house had yellow walls and green pillars. I knocked on the front door. There was a garden gnome underneath the front window, and a hat upside-down beside the mat. *Welcome*, the mat still said. A woman in overalls and fluffy blonde hair set in two messy bunches on the sides of her head pulled the door open in one swift movement.

I kept waiting to see some resemblance. Max had thick curly black hair, huge blue eyes, pretty lashes. I stared at the poor woman for definitely too long, not seeing any resemblance, or any possibility that a woman this age had once had a teenager for a son.

Finally, I said, 'I thought this was Max's house. My name's Bridie. We went to school together.'

'Oh.' Her mouth, too, made the shape of an O, as round as a frying pan. 'I'm his mum's friend. She moved away.'

'Oh.'

'I'm going to help sell this house for her – know anyone?'

'No.'

'I was kidding,' she said. She narrowed her eyes at me. 'Kids don't get jokes anymore, do they?'

That's not a joke, lady, I thought. But instead I shrugged.

'I'm Louise,' she said. 'Wanna sit?'

She pointed to a long, narrow wooden bench beneath one of the windows overlooking the verandah. She stretched out her legs on the seat. She tugged at her sock, then started unlacing her sneakers. There wasn't much room left for me, so I dropped my backpack at my feet and took up just one end.

'What can I help you with, Bridie?'

'I won some money.'

'That's cool. How'd you do that?'

I told Louise about Mrs Eames and the fruit flies. She wanted to know what some of the other entries looked like. I wondered how old Louise was. Thirty? Forty? She said congratulations. She sounded like she meant it.

'Thanks.'

'What are you going to do with the cash?' she asked.

I inhaled deeply. 'I was going to give it to Max's mum.'

These temptations, why couldn't I stop them? Misery coursed through me. Mrs Eames hadn't failed me since the piece was for an award, and not for classwork, but she disqualified me from the show. And, of course, she now thought less of me. And Louise might very well say, *Yes, okay, great, hand it over.* And then what? What would I do, having not at all won the money?

Louise stopped what she was doing with her socks and shoes, and she stared at me, hands held up. 'Look, I understand if you're sad. What happened was awful. But I used to work with Max's mother, that's all. I said I'd help her with the house for a while.'

'I'm serious about the money. I've never known anyone who died. Maybe at school we weren't that nice to him. I'm trying to make things up to people.'

'That's really sweet of you.' She swung her legs to the floor and smiled at me for the first time. 'But there's no need.'

'I'm not trolling you,' I said. 'I've been thinking about Max. Mostly about his family, how they won't get any peace from now on.'

Louise cocked her head and studied me like Mrs Eames had. Even Klara, it felt like she spent more time watching me, and me alone, than Nick or any of the others that day.

My words rushed out: 'But also, I led him on. I kind of pretended I liked him and wanted to sleep with him, but then I rejected him. I was pretty mean.'

'Oh, love.' She said this tenderly. 'We all did bad things at school.'

If she didn't have kids, Louise would have made a really nice mother. She stood and ran her hands down the front of her overalls, brushing at nothing that I could see. 'It was good of you to come over,' she said. 'Don't worry about his mum. Okay?'

~

Nick's mother, she sits me down in her fancy kitchen, she wants to tell me something. I seize up: she must have figured out the real me, and I'll be exposed in the sharp light reflected off the benchtop. But what she says is that being young is wonderful. She says adults are always looking forwards or backwards to before they had kids, or into the future when their kids are all grown up and they're free again. So, to counter this, Nick's mother is really trying to work on being in the moment, with her two beautiful boys and the ages they are right now before they head off into the big wide world. I stop myself from asking what she thinks Richie will end up doing, because she seems so radiant, and so hopeful, and so loving towards me. Cubes of ice clink in her glass. She asks if I want one. I do. We have a cold white wine each. I wish I had a cigarette to hold between my fingertips for these ten minutes while Nick gets the washing off the line for his mother. We are two women sitting legs crossed with our bodies towards each other, speaking with our knees.

TITAN ARUM

2004 | LINDA B. BUCK | PHYSIOLOGY OR MEDICINE

Prize motivation: 'for their discoveries of odorant receptors and the organization of the olfactory system'

THE BAGS THEY'D PACKED AND brought from home were in the spare bedroom with its pair of single beds and red doona covers and cushions. Grandma, like always, had taken their pyjamas out and set them on top of their pillows. Emily appreciated this touch. She and her older brother, Tyler, hadn't been given a lot of time to pack, their mum not knowing how long they'd be here for, but probably just for a bit. Probably just till the end of the week. Emily's school dress was hanging in the wardrobe; her school shoes were there, too, in case it tipped into next week when the holidays were over. She slipped off her socks and tucked them beneath her bed.

She heard her brother yelling out for her. He always insisted he had cooler, better people to play with, but he always called for her.

She wandered back through the house, thinking about Milo, the dog they'd had to put down a few years ago because they discovered his hips had not been developing in the right way. Their mother brought the ashes back here, to Emily's grandparents' house, and buried them. That's what Mum told them.

Emily found Tyler standing in the mud in a far corner of the huge front yard. She knew Grandma and Grandpa never came out here. It would take some doing, some hacking through branches and clumps of thick ferns. Her grandma had never cared about gardening so she wasn't all of a sudden about to start weeding on her knees. Her grandpa seemed to have lots of tools in the garage, but he mostly stayed inside now.

Tyler poked at the flower, which was huge, the hugest they had ever seen. They'd noticed the plant before. But never like this, never in bloom. It stood as tall as Emily and was pale green, a colour sort of like the Hulk, with a frilly red-and-green skirt.

'Whoa,' Tyler said. 'I've heard about these. It's half-human and half-plant.'

'It stinks.'

'It was on David Attenborough,' he said. 'There's a chance it's going to grow legs – a pretty strong chance – and eat you up at night.'

'I don't believe you,' Emily said, scrunching up her face. There. When had there ever been such an easy solution?

'I think – I *think* I remember Attenborough saying – it can't come inside,' Tyler said. 'So you should be okay.'

For half a second at the most, she had wondered. She looked at her brother. Even he seemed to know he'd gone too far with the plant having hands and somehow fingers and somehow a key for their grandparents' house. She glanced again at the flower.

Tyler kicked at the wet earth. 'Do you dare me to put my head right in it?'

'Yes,' Emily said.

'You dare me?'

'I dare you.'

But before Tyler could claim victory, Emily stomped right up and did it. Then the smell. Her brain went all animal. She was nothing but nose. The smell was a solid thing in her throat that she coughed at. Nappies stacked in a bin and left in the sun. The downstairs toilet an hour after breakfast. Dead possums on the bitumen. She stumbled back and screeched. 'Grandpa!'

~

Brooks woke in his favourite armchair. The clock said three, a bit after. He heard the voices of his grandchildren playing in the yard. He was seventy-nine years old, and pretty much anything he wanted out of life now had to come to him. There would be no driving to the base of a mountain and then walking up it and back down again, or suddenly learning to snowboard. Brooks burped and touched his chest. For a second he panicked about the children, and if they were safe. Then he heard his name being called. He would have to steady himself and go find them.

By the time he and Kathleen met the man who their daughter, Rose, had decided was good enough for her – *bam!* – she was six months pregnant and already thinking about the next one. Craving cucumbers and handfuls of lettuce from the back garden of the old house, a few years before they moved here. Can't be that bad, he'd thought, getting yourself pregnant with a baby that makes you crave salad twelve hours a day. She could not stand the smell of coffee, or meat frying on the stove, so Kathleen stopped making those things. Instead she knitted their daughter bunny rugs, while Rose lay on the sofa, her round and pretty head in Brooks's lap. And while his wife knitted, Brooks had looked at her over their daughter's horizontal body. They were careful not to talk about W---, even when Rose was not in the room, but especially not then and there with Brooks at one end of the couch and Kathleen sitting in an armchair at the other end. Rose's eyes were closed. He wanted to lean down and smell her hair. Kathleen's eyes said, *Don't talk about W---* and Brooks's eyes yelled back, *I wasn't going to. I would never!* W--- keeping tabs on her in the way he did. Things would only get worse. Taking the kids out of school early to go on a roadtrip to the coast and ringing Rose at work to say they were crying for her, that they were being bad. Rose having to scramble to leave the office, get on the highway, reach W--- on the phone to find out his exact location in peak-hour traffic. Sometimes he'd go all cool after that, after she'd already taken emergency leave from her work, W---'s particular brand that had you wondering if you'd made the whole thing up. *Everything's fine. I'll bring the kids home later.*

Brooks didn't know people could be like that. He'd never in all his years as a draughtsman, then a civil engineer – he must have met hundreds of men, especially – met anyone as exacting and cruel as W---. It baffled him. One day, after Rose had broken it off again in a way that seemed final, W--- sneaked up on her in the big underground car park of her office, his face appearing at her window. Smiling and tap-tapping on the glass with his knuckles. The way Rose had told it there'd been no-one else around. Brooks still had moments, even now, five years later, when he imagined what he would do – summoning some force that was not his – with his hand on the back of W---'s head. *Bam.* Into the door of his daughter's car. Not enough to kill him. But something.

Brooks stood up from the chair, eventually, into the haze of the kitchen. Kathleen had forgotten to put on the exhaust fan once again. The fatty stench of sausages and the sweet, sharp scent of fried onions were in the air. The remains of cut sandwiches sat on melamine plates on the table – Rose's dulled and scratched Winnie-the-Pooh ones from childhood.

A cry caught in his throat. Their lovely baby daughter who used to fall asleep easier if he patted her rump had fallen in love with a real deadshit. That was a tragedy nobody could prepare you for. And now Rose's own son and daughter were playing in the front yard, the rain having finally stopped after forty-eight hours straight. Not great timing, he was now realising – having two kids, one twelve and one eight, stay at your house for who knows how long, both of them loving to run and move. Which seemed to be all they wanted to do. Brooks gripped the back of a kitchen chair – one he had built himself when they were first married. There must have been a time when he used to run and move in a way that was not painstakingly planned. He turned to the window where he saw his granddaughter gesturing to him, asking him to follow her. The sky was clear. Her face said he should hurry.

~

Emily grabbed her grandfather by the hand, telling him that he had to see this. It was the grossest thing she'd ever seen, ever smelt. She was kind of excited by it all, kind of couldn't wait to get back there and do it again. He took some dragging, and was really slow, but finally she got him past the birdbath and the clothesline and round to the front of the house.

'It's in here,' she said. 'Watch your head. Can you do it?'

Tyler came out through the thickest, most jungly part to meet them. 'Are you going to be able to get through?'

Their grandfather placed his hands on the sides of his face. Emily knew that once upon a time he'd scored a double century against Souths on the hottest day of the year. Once, when their mother was a toddler, he'd carried her on his back all the way home from Central Station.

'Come on,' Emily said, reaching for him. And he held her arm gently in his great big dry hand, which felt nice.

'Holy shit!' Tyler said. 'Sorry. But, whoa. Grandpa, can you smell that?'

Emily watched her grandfather look around this corner of the garden – seeming, sure enough, as though he hadn't been here in ages. He blinked behind his glasses till he followed Tyler's arm to where he was pointing wildly at the flower. If it were possible, the smell had got even worse. Tyler pulled his t-shirt up over his mouth and nose.

Emily had never heard her grandfather swear.

~

Now out in the garage, Brooks closed his eyes to try to remember where it might be kept now. Years since he'd needed the thing. He leaned against a workbench and seized the bulk of the old black vice to steady himself.

Smells from the kerosene lamp and fuel for the lawn mower zapped into his nose. That time he'd taught Rose to mow the lawn: his daughter begging him to teach her, not the other way round. Kids shouldn't be put to work, had been his feeling. The time he lit a fire in a drum and set it under the patio of the old house for Rose and her little friends to toast the marshmallows they'd planned on doing in the backyard. An at-home camping trip with tents? Something like that. But it had rained? Just like it had rained today, and yesterday. Rose and her friends' shining faces so amazed at his fire-making ability. One of them offered him the first marshmallow she made. *Quick! Before it droops, Mr O'Neill!*

What a fool that W--- was to waste all that. To destroy any chance of being Teach Me Things Dad or Hero Dad or even just Stay Out Of The Way Dad, like when Rose became a teenager and her friends came to visit. Beautiful young Emily, well, he could show her things, if his mind stayed put and his back stopped playing up.

He let go of the vice.

He remembered that cousin of Kathleen's who'd been putting up with a bad back for ages. Turned out: cancer. So Brooks stopped telling Kathleen about the worst of his pain. God, how a thing goes from a bad back to cancer in ten seconds flat is anybody's guess. Until he figured out what he would do if that were indeed the cause, well, he'd very much stay mum on that subject.

Other garage smells now, other memories. It felt good to have things percolating in his brain. The blackened, metallic scent of the tools lined up on his workbench. The day, sometime before Tyler was born, when Rose had asked him to find something from her childhood that the baby might want, when he'd hauled out the plastic tubs and emptied them on the lawn, digging through, when hope was still a bright thing in his chest because W--- was keeping himself in check and behaving more like a protective and good guy than what he later turned out to be. What was it he had found? A bouncer, one of those old skinny metal ones shaped like a horseshoe, over which you stretched a cottony cover. Babies couldn't get enough of those things. He and Kathleen would have loved to buy the baby a new one, but Rose recycled and didn't eat meat so he had trusted that this was what she'd wanted.

~

Emily opened the screen door and made her way around to the other side of the house. From the front of the garage, she watched her grandfather at work. His hair, which was loose and grey, bounced each time he moved. She would have liked to hear him whistle. Adults did that when things were good. The clock above the beer fridge showed the time. The dartboard was still punctured with the darts she and Tyler had stuck in it yesterday, walking right up and pressing them in, because who was going to stop them? Over and over. Pair after pair of perfect scores. They'd high-fived each other, then grabbed cans of ginger ale from the fridge to drink before their grandmother told them dinner was ready. Dinner was ready super early in this house, but it didn't matter if you got hungry again because Grandma put on dessert right after dinner, and then supper with biscuits and a cup of tea a bit after that.

They'd be here one night, maybe two. Unlikely to be more than four. That was how her mother spoke. Started off making sense then got lost somewhere along the way.

'Grandpa? Phone for you. It's my mum.'

He stopped whatever it was he was doing – she couldn't see it. He turned to her. He had eyes the colour of gravel.

'Thanks, sweetheart.' He was waiting for her to hand over the phone.

Emily noticed tins of paint. She cast a critical eye over a mound of oily cloths and twists of what looked like toilet paper with black grease running through them. Then she handed him the phone.

'Hello?' Grandpa said. He glanced at Emily. 'Rose? Hello?'

'Actually,' Emily said, coming up close to him and whispering now. 'She didn't ring. But can you do that? Can you tell her to not be ages? Please?'

He ran a hand through his hair and put the phone down on the workbench. 'Let her get where she's going, Em. Give her a chance to ring us first.'

~

The kids were yelling and hollering and carrying on. There could be days if not weeks of this, god love them. Brooks was worse at the hands-on stuff than his wife. When the kids were toddlers, Kathleen used to hoick them out of the bath and run a towel over them. Knickers, shirt, pants, all done in thirty seconds flat.

Days ago, Rose had given Kathleen a look when she'd asked how long Rose might be gone, a look that meant there would be no clear answer but that she loved Tyler and Emily more than the world. A look that said, *Do not ask me if I've gone off to see W---.* And Brooks and Kathleen's reply, also without words, while Kathleen stroked their daughter's hand across the kitchen tabletop was, *Such a thing would break our hearts.* All their eyes agreed: *Let's keep that man as happy as can be because we fear what he might do one day.* They wished he never existed, but that would mean no Emily and Tyler.

It had been on-again, off-again with W--- for so long. His great big grin at Emily's christening party when Brooks's sister, Anne, watched him take a tray of brownies out of the oven. Anne had flown in and had only just met him, but she'd heard Brooks's stories. She said, *Those brownies were ready a long time ago. He was waiting for someone to notice him open the oven.* She told Brooks to tell Rose to break it off.

But they could not make her do that.

'Emily!'

'You do it!' or something like that.

Emily now, the voices of his grandchildren rising and carrying to him again across the yard in the late afternoon. Kathleen – he heard her too, in a tone like she was trying to placate them. Tired. Their voices gripped him, shook him. Distress settled into him like spadefuls of dirt in the earth.

He searched the house for the phone and when he finally found it on Emily's pillow, he tried his daughter's number. It rang and rang then clicked in for a sliver of Rose's voice – *Hi, you've reached* – and he hung up. He tried again. And again and again.

Before his back could seize up, he strode to the garage, got the machete, held it vertically down the side of his right leg and moved swiftly across the yard. Past the birdbath and the clothesline. He sort of noticed how Emily and Tyler scattered to make way for him. Their faces, which were little repeating sequences of Rose's, opened in surprise. Kathleen started to speak, but Brooks didn't stop to listen. He brought the machete up behind his shoulder and rained blows upon the flower. Not watching to see what Kathleen was warning him about. Hoping the kids thought everything was fine.

THE BODIES ARE BURIED

2008 | FRANÇOISE BARRÉ-SINOUSSI | PHYSIOLOGY OR MEDICINE

Prize motivation: 'for their discovery of human immunodeficiency virus'

2015

FIONA WATCHED HER DAUGHTER, LIVI, CLOSELY. Livi followed her father around like a moonshadow. She presented him with gifts: beads on a string, triangles of coloured paper stuffed in an envelope, a clay bowl filled with paper clips and coins.

Marcus glanced at Fiona then back at Livi. 'Is this for Mummy?'

'No, it's for you.'

Take up your position as the second-best-loved parent. Want a baby very badly. In the years after that, try hard to do right by your child, even though – despite the fact that – a little oily thrum in the centre of your being says, *It's actually a bum deal, this motherhood gig.* Try to keep it from your daughter; find out that this is impossible. Livi, for example, seemed to have a keen sense of everything her mother tried to hide: the brutal, bloody TV shows; chocolate biscuits in the pantry; sex with Marcus sitting up in bed in the early morning. The sneakiest part of herself met the sneakiest part of her daughter, and both became immovable.

2030

Around the world, things were starting to look grim. Now was not the time to have a baby. At the clinic on the edge of the city where Fiona had booked Livi's abortion, Fiona held Livi's hand and for once her daughter let her. A woman at the counter passed over a clipboard and pen. Fiona waited for Livi to take it, but she didn't. They sat together on chairs. In the waiting room were another mother and daughter, even younger than Livi. Plus two more women sitting close together, sharp white collars beneath black blazers. Straight from the office, Fiona thought.

Her own mud-spattered ute was parked on the street outside. She couldn't figure out the city parking meter and Livi got so cross that Fiona ended up scrawling a sad, hick note that she left on the dash: *From out of town and couldn't work machine. Sorry. Promise to pay.*

'This will become a memory,' Fiona said, ticking boxes on the form, not looking at her daughter. 'Trust me. I had you so young. You'll thank me.'

'I will not thank you.' She shifted to show Fiona her face mottled with pink splotches. 'God, Mum.'

'You'll lay down other memories. Better ones.'

'When?' The way she said *when*: Livi was a tiny girl once more, desperate to get her ears pierced. To get a part-time job. To be allowed to hitchhike into Toowoomba alongside the road trains on the Warrego.

'Someday. It's a bum deal, this motherhood gig.'

Livi spoke, but Fiona wasn't listening. She paused and rested the end of the pen on her daughter's arm. 'Sorry, love?'

'I said, you've told me a million times.'

2032

Fiona invited Livi onto the back steps one night after Marcus had moved out. (All absurdly amicable. Marcus promised to keep in touch, even coming back to replace the ceramic planter he'd broken on moving day. After he closed the truck door, they found themselves awkwardly hugging.) Each evening since the separation, Fiona had felt herself relax, here in the house they'd cared about so much for decades.

Livi sat cross-legged on the cold concrete across from Fiona, not touching. Finally, when Livi spoke, she told her that she was heading overseas in a month. She'd booked a ticket on impulse, no surprises there, *haha*. Backpacking.

Fiona's first thought was that something bad was going to happen to her daughter. Her second thought was that the family home was emptying out by thirds and she loved it.

'Go,' she told Livi. *Yes.* 'This is what I meant for you to do all along. Have *fun*. Keep safe.'

Fiona could eat soup every night and wash up just the one spoon. One bowl. She remembered thinking this, about the bowl. That's where her mind had gone, gleefully.

2034

Livi called Fiona, the ring catching her while she was packing up her kitchen. She plunged her hands into the pockets of her fat parka, searching for a tissue. She dug around in her bra – her late mother had always kept tissues in her bra to hand over to whoever needed one. She blew her nose away from the phone. Nights were cold. Where she was moving – back west to the family Queenslander in the Lockyer Valley – would be even colder.

Fiona folded the tissue to tuck into her sleeve. 'Love, it's wonderful to hear from you. Feeling better this week?'

The membrane of the tissue between her fingers while her daughter delivered the news. *HIV.*

'Wait. What did you say?'

Livi didn't want to talk about how she got it or where. She'd be coming home. But not immediately. Fiona's mind cracked a little.

Forcefully, brightly, Livi said she would tell her one day, but for now Fiona didn't need to know.

2042

The pub was new. Well, the renovation was. Fiona tossed her handbag over the back of a chair. She waved to her sometime-boss, Kelman. She gave a hoy to the new school teacher in town. She wandered to the bar and patted down her hair. A stranger tapped the freshly buffed pine in front of her. He had close-shorn white hair with a large bald patch on top and a neat beard. She ordered herself a beer before he could offer, which she understood he wanted to do. Fiona knew country men and pubs.

They exchanged small talk for five minutes, then ten minutes, till the man – Tom was his name – said, 'Looking to date anyone?' Tom had a flat, slightly teasing voice. But his eyes were kind.

Fiona made a show of lifting her glass off the bar and swivelling around towards the tables and chairs as if to say, *Get a load of this bloke.* But no-one glanced up, and Tom met her gaze truthfully, and not jokingly.

Did she want to *date* anyone?

Sure, she thought, sure she could. She had time. The house didn't require a lot from her. Her work kept her busy, but not that busy. She was making a living back in her childhood district, working on her neighbours' farms. She checked irrigation pumps. She was diligent and instinctive. Had common sense. People trusted her with their stock. She got her hands dirty often, but hers was a job for someone organised and meticulous. Fiona was a good thinker. She thought of Livi, who hadn't told her the specifics of the insemination procedure (or *procedures* if they weren't lucky the first time) and how they went about it these days. Fair enough. She wasn't much of a nurturer. But if Livi had asked her along for moral support, Fiona would have listened and not asked anything embarrassing. And been careful not to get her hopes up about a grandchild.

She smiled at Tom. 'I have a daughter. She's the love of my life.' Saying it caught her by surprise. This wasn't how she usually talked, had never used that expression before.

'Hard for a man to compete *et cetera et cetera*,' he said, enunciating each syllable in a way Fiona knew was protective, ironic.

She realised she'd been unkind. She was being unkind in this very moment, squinting at this stranger while he *enunciated* so dreadfully with a sliver of peanut shell stuck between his two front teeth. He looked suddenly old, which meant so did she. Her mind turned to Livi.

'It probably is,' she said. 'Cheers.'

'Okay, then,' he said. 'Cheers.'

2045

Fiona was driving west to the Kelman property to begin her day. She pulled in at the bakery where Kelman's wife worked. Faded Cornetto signs and vintage teapots along one wall, and humming Coke fridges and a flat screen tuned to a weather channel on the other. Fiona pointed to a lamington, asked Shelley about the family.

'Lachlan – the oldest grandson – his latest thought is doing theatre at uni,' Shelley said, handing over a paper bag. 'If he gets the marks.'

'I did theatre,' Fiona said, surprising herself. Another slice of her life that seemed to belong to another person.

'You did? When?'

'Oh, Shell, I don't know. A million years ago.'

'Was it wild?'

'God, no. The opposite, I think. We were all quite conservative.'

One semester, their new tutor was young and trendy Graeme, who wore black button-up shirts and something he referred to as 'loafers'. He came in to guide the class through a documentary drama. At the time, they were all the rage. Graeme had just returned from subjecting locals in Africa to Augusto Boal. Here in the heart of Brisbane, 2003, their documentary drama would be about HIV. Graeme wanted Fiona's playbuilding class to talk about sex and bodies and desire. Fiona felt like screaming, *I'm from Mulgowie!* He plunged the classroom into darkness and told them to move and touch, *move and touch*, whatever they came up against. Elbow. Knee. Neck. Fingers, cheeks, thigh. Fiona figured out her friends in the dark. She knew it was their laughter she could hear. Six-and-a-half-foot Robert over on the mechanical tiered seating, unable to control his stomping even then. Bec shaking with giggles behind the curtain – if she didn't move she couldn't be touched, was probably what she was thinking.

Fiona had dropped low to the ground, framing the hour-long workshop in her mind, how she and the others would take it apart later over Fanta and hot chips. Cracking up, appalled, so embarrassed. They were easily embarrassed, every last one of them. But one girl in particular, strident Natasha, half-ignored by the class and already engaged to be married to her boring boyfriend, sought out a senior lecturer and put a stop to the whole thing. They never saw Graeme again, and the class performed a dreadful last-minute *Taming of the Shrew* instead.

What prigs we were, Fiona thought. She felt sorry for that young man. She didn't think that would happen now, with students. Was everyone a prude? Maybe not. But today's lecturers were probably too afraid to try.

'Do you wish you still did it?'

'What? Pardon, sorry?'

'Did you ...' White-haired Shelley skipped out from behind the cash register and performed a flamboyant bow to show Fiona what she meant. An audience of one. 'Drama? Did you continue with it?'

The idea was so ridiculous Fiona laughed.

Milk for the lambs, creamy as paint. Fiona took the bottles, one in each hand and the third in the wide pocket of her overalls. She fed them, relishing the suck of their mouths at the teats. Their single-minded vigour. After they had eaten, she closed the creatures up in their pens. Her phone was back in the ute. She'd have liked to take a photo of the smallest lamb with its face scrunched up and pressed into the wire to send to Livi and little Heidi, who took a filthy pink lamb blankie to bed each night, sleeping with its rump in her mouth. Another time.

The feeding done, she set off along the gravel road back towards the car. The hills looked fat and green as tennis balls. She stopped for a moment to take it all in. The lushness was bright against the thick, dark grey lard of the low clouds. Half-a-dozen farmhouses that she'd seen twice a day from the windows of the bus to school and then home again, all those years ago when she was a teenager and she'd barely registered the world around her. Now she noticed the abandoned red chassis in the front yard of one, and the boarded-up windows of another. And then it began to rain. The pelt of the raindrops pocked against the heavy fabric of her overalls. She ducked her head and pictured the distance to the ute. A crack of thunder and an enormous downpour. Nothing to do but keep running, walking when her left knee began to hurt. The lambs were penned in and cocooned in their waxy coats. Livi and Heidi were far away, but safe; she knew they were safe.

The rain was clearing when she reached Kelman's. The last light drops were in her hair and on her face. Fiona lifted her boots in and out of the wet earth with a suck like the lambs at their teats. She walked to the edge of the yard.

Mud all around. The old shitty ute was bogged.

'Fuck,' she said. She had the other paddocks to do, the Muller lambs to check on, and the pumps out on Hanover Road, and past the old Donaghy property. Fuck, again, a cruel berating herself this time, for parking here and not somewhere higher. A hard, round fury at Kelman for keeping his yard such a mess.

She pulled on the driver-side door and was unsurprised when it was as immovable as a wall. But the passenger door opened and she lifted herself onto the seat. She flung the mail, chip packets, a handful of pencils onto the floor so her bum would fit. No point even trying to shift the tyres. She reached Kelman on his mobile. He said he'd be there in half an hour, maybe three-quarters. He joked about women drivers, told her to sit tight and not go anywhere – she gave him a brief laugh for this. In a gentler voice he asked how the lambs were.

'Nothing to report,' she said. She was trying to get off the phone.

'All right, all right, you don't need me. Be there soon. Give us a hoy if anything changes,' he said.

Standing at the bakery with Shelley earlier, well, Fiona had left out one bit.

Before their class project went kaput, Graeme had driven Fiona and three others to the Queensland AIDS Council, a house with a sunny, sloping backyard up near the Mater Hospital. Graeme wanted the students to talk to people who worked at the house and who got help there. A man made them cups of tea. They sat in the backyard on warm wooden benches, facing the house. Fiona and her friends were nervous, but not the men. *So you want to know how we got here?* one of them asked. He was young and handsome, wearing a t-shirt printed with the name of a band Fiona had wanted to like. Another man was older, skinnier, paler. Fiona was clueless about the illness, but she was a good listener. Graeme must have sensed this. She barely said a word the whole visit. The old man took a sip from his mug. Smiling, he faced Fiona: *You want to know about the bodies we've buried.*

Mud all around and no panic in her now. She had a sausage roll in the esky and half the lamington if Kelman was late. A litre of dusty water in an orange juice bottle was at her feet if she got desperate.

Then Fiona remembered the photos Livi had sent her earlier in the day when she'd been too busy to check properly. She levered off her muddy boots and rested her head against the window. She opened the message. No text, just four photos of her beaming granddaughter. One with her chubby legs stuck inside the black rubber of a swing. One of Heidi lifting sand in fistfuls towards the camera. Heidi kneeling on the playground lawn, showering her pink lamb with blades of grass. Heidi gripping a low tree branch, proud of her tentative steps while she edged around it and towards her mother, who held the camera just out of reach.

BETTER NATURE

2009 | ADA E. YONATH | CHEMISTRY

Prize motivation: 'for studies of the structure and function of the ribosome'

WE WENT TO THE GOOD Japanese restaurant in Camden Town. The waiter took my coat with such care and gentleness that I wondered if he knew I was pregnant. Clearly absurd since I was barely showing – still, gentleness had a way of making me cry. Of exhausting me. The restaurant looked less impressive than the last time I'd been there, six months earlier with my colleagues from the lab, celebrating the occasion of Olga's boyfriend getting his indefinite leave to remain approved. My mother wouldn't like the closeness of the tables, would be paranoid about people eavesdropping. The violet downlights and dull black faux-leather banquettes now gave me the vibe of an airport bar. Which all reminded me: my mother and father had flown from Queensland to London to take me home.

I stopped inside the front door. 'Is this going to be okay?' I asked.

Mum and Dad sort of ran into my back – an accidental slapstick routine. Dad unwound his scarf and got tangled in it. The handsome, youthful waiter holding our menus glanced away. He was being a good sport.

'It's perfect,' I answered myself. I mouthed *Oh, god* then *Thank you* at the poor man.

We sat, and I ordered quickly for everyone. I couldn't bear to watch while my parents made the waiter answer their questions about daikon and how the hotpots worked. I added that we'd need a couple of forks. Immediately, I felt uncharitable. A total bitch. I tipped over to my mother next to me on the banquette and kissed her on the cheek.

'The snow!' Mum said, beaming. 'We looked out of the hotel window at about four o'clock and saw this beautiful whooshing outside. Is it normal for March?'

'I don't think so,' I said.

'Ah, we must be lucky,' Dad said.

I had long ago realised that Dad – who grew up in a nothing town with ordinary routines and quiet work and not much to look forward to – had experienced an entire life that must have felt triumphant, and very joyful. If I became a school teacher after all this had blown over, which was most likely, I might lead a quiet life too. Julian would paint landscapes in some country town, standing on a ridge with a palette and a jar of water. But even I could see – three seconds after having it – this bucolic fantasy for what it was, and I stifled a chuckle.

'Nothing,' I said, when they stared. 'Sorry. Just thinking.'

I fiddled with the lacquered chopsticks, sending them back and forth through my fingers. When the food arrived, I dug ravenously into a bowl of udon.

'Absolutely delicious, Maddy,' Dad said. 'Thank you.'

'Oh. Yes.' I said. 'This is my shout.'

Mum scoffed. 'Absolutely not.'

'I insist. After all I've put you through.'

Dad cleared his throat and speared a piece of tempura sweet potato with his fork. 'What do you think ... how will you tell Joanna? Have you spoken to her lately?'

I knew what he was doing. 'No.'

He was ready for my answer. 'She's your sister.'

'It might be nice to try again,' Mum said. Strategically, she sipped from her glass of red.

The waiter brought over a gleaming platter of ice topped with sashimi arranged on bundles of twigs. I stared at it before realising I was the one who had ordered it, forgetting I was pregnant. I knew it would go uneaten, and that nice waiter would be left wondering what was wrong with the food.

'Well' – Mum pinched at her lips like she was trying to coax out a smile – 'I'm sure you'll reconnect when you're back home.' She leaned in. 'When there's a *baby*.'

'Give it time,' Dad said, nodding. He sank his fork into his bowl of rice.

'Is there any recourse?' Mum asked. I bristled at this formal word I'd never heard her use before. 'Higher up than this one lab supervisor?'

'Don't think so!' I said brightly. 'I'm leaving, aren't I? I think it's a done deal.'

'I'd imagine they don't take too fondly to things like that,' Dad said.

Things like that. The things I had done unknowingly. The things I had done out of pressure, out of desperation. The results I was sure I could replicate, given the right lab conditions and the right colleagues. The things I felt blameless for. The academic rules I knew I had broken, willingly. Things like that.

I kept dreaming of smoking. I was in an unfamiliar house with lights on in the windows. Party guests who I remembered from high-school soccer were there, but they loomed larger, softer, older. I sensed there was a carton of cigarettes in the house – meant for me – all I had to do was find it. I searched in the hallstand drawer and in the kitchen cupboards. I did this stealthily. To at least one person I lied about what I was doing. Then I was on the street, out the front, all traffic disappeared from sight and sound. I was alone with the dancing, lit tip of a cigarette and I breathed it in. When I woke, my fingers were in the shape of a V on the pillow. Julian's boots at the door, the smell of bacon frying on a hotplate down the hall. When I told Julian about the dream, about how guilty I felt, he said, 'It's just a dream, baby. Breathe.'

Before Christmas Julian had some still lifes and a few landscapes hung at a gallery above the Lion and Unicorn. In our last few days together, he searched for reviews of the show in the student papers till it was clear there would be no reviews, good or bad.

I marvelled at my body when I saw my reflection in a window on the way to the Tube. Julian stroked my belly, and we searched online for apartments in Sydney that we could perhaps afford together one day. Six hundred and fifty dollars a week, shared backyard, no storage, no garage. Etc, etc. Till his Australian visa got approved, I'd live with Mum and Dad.

Julian and I sat on the floor of our studio in Battersea and packed my things into big cartons – 'tea chests', the shipping company called them.

I stood up. 'Help me get in.'

'Pardon?'

'As a joke. Help me in.'

I set it upright on the floor beside the bed. I climbed onto the mattress, Julian held my hand and I sort of slid my legs into the box. I crouched at its base, cradling my belly in the dark.

'Close the lid,' I told him.

Later on, I labelled the cartons in permanent marker on every side, as the company instructed, with my parents' address. I hoped Mum and Dad would have room for all my crap, for the few childhood things I had brought with me to London, that they could now have back.

At Heathrow, the PA system blared, and baristas called out unrecognisable names and a perfume lady tried to grab my hand. Mum and Dad gave us time alone while they pretended to shop for headphones and duty-free gin for Joanna.

Julian and I stood face to face. He undid his coat and fitted it around our bodies. I wanted so badly to believe my boyfriend, who insisted this was temporary and cinematic in a cross-cultural northern-hemisphere-southern-hemisphere kind of way.

'This is horrible,' I whispered. 'This is the worst thing. How is this happening?'

I was half-awake in our house on the Gold Coast, in my half-made room. Whenever I started to unpack the boxes, I had to lie down with the doona wrapped tight around my shoulders. I couldn't quite believe where I had been, and what I'd been forced to do. *No-one forced you to do anything*, the Joanna-in-my-head said. Shame had taken root inside me. The sooner this baby was out, the better. I had been in that city, and in that world with my famous, fearsome supervisor and her loyal group of laser-focused students. And now I wasn't. When the other girls in my lab and I went for Japanese, we would have looked for all the world like an advertisement for shiny, brainy multiculturalism. Namita and Olga and Tali, the bold ones who got us tables at popular places when we hadn't thought to book ahead. Then Maja and me with our arms linked, lagging behind. A week after I was fired, Olga emailed me a huge, meandering treatise that gradually got blunter and blunter in her assessment of me. At the end she wrote, *You fabricated our results. I can't see a different solution, can you?* On my birthday last month, Namita texted me a gif of a ginger cat holding a balloon. Nothing from the others.

As I lay on my side, getting overheated, stuffing a pillow between my legs for comfort, a different memory began to muss about in my brain. I was fifteen, in hospital after having my appendix removed, and my father and sister had come to visit. I hadn't realised the pain I'd be in or how difficult walking would be. I asked Joanna to help me shower in the ensuite beyond the curtain.

'I'll stay here,' Dad said, standing up to pass me my overnight bag.

The loveliness of stepping through the door and then behind the shower curtain with my older sister on the other side, holding that wretched catheter bag. I knew she would see me naked, catch glimpses of parts of me she hadn't seen in years. I felt Joanna's quiet patience behind the blue vinyl while I tried to soap my underarms, my breasts, between my legs with one hand. The sheer relief of being upright and clean with my sister at the end of the line, passing me first the sponge then a hard white hospital face washer. She picked up on the patter of my words – the food had been fine, the pain hadn't stopped, there were some good magazines in the TV room – and fell silent when I did too. When I was about to turn off the taps and ask for my towel, Dad started singing a couple of bars of a song that was popular at the time. He'd forgotten where he was, perhaps, or he needed something to cut through the slight discomfort of his two daughters in the bathroom together. I imagined him slapping the arms of his chair to the beat. Joanna and I both let out gasps of laughter, softly, so he wouldn't be deterred. Water from my shower beaded up and down her sleeve.

It was a tender memory and it sliced down upon me now, back in my childhood bed after moving overseas then failing at so many things and being forced to come home. I felt the baby in all its readiness to be born, giving me a kick like a shout.

'Joanna!' I cried out. 'Julian!'

WINGSPAN

2009 | ELIZABETH H. BLACKBURN | PHYSIOLOGY OR MEDICINE

Prize motivation: 'for the discovery of how chromosomes are protected by telomeres and the enzyme telomerase'

ELIZABETH

SPRING IN LAUNCESTON, LATE OCTOBER, and Elizabeth sat on the floor in the hallway, waiting for her friend Wendy to arrive. The sound of her mother opening drawers in the kitchen travelled across the lounge room. Upstairs, her brother, Benjamin, sang in his room, a hymn from church – words Elizabeth hadn't believed in for months. A sad song. But Elizabeth could rely on Wendy to lift her mood, to talk underwater, to be a great guest for a party, which would start tonight at Elizabeth's house. All day there'd been excitement, thrills rushing through her body. This afternoon: Wendy. Later: Miss Loveling. Tonight: her Uncle Gordon, the pilot.

She had to prepare her bedroom for Wendy's arrival. Elizabeth enjoyed observing her own generosity with her friend: a spiritual flinging open of her bedroom door to show Wendy her desk, the toys she had kept since she was a baby, the clothes in her wardrobe, and some but not all of her treasures under the bed.

From her spot on the floor, Elizabeth glanced up at the staircase behind her, but her room seemed far away, requiring so much energy, and someone was sure to come along the minute she rose and start to speak at her simply because they saw movement. Her stillness here was breeding its own stillness across the house.

But. There was work to do.

On the duchess in her bedroom, Elizabeth found the hairpins she'd been looking for that morning. The heavy volume her father had given her called *Malady: A Dictionary of Medical Words and Phrases* sat open on her bed to an illustration of the mature ovum. On her desk were two pencil boxes in which all the greens, reds, browns and blues were worn down to nubs. Underneath these sat a paintbox that she couldn't bear to use. It was certainly too good – her mother said it cost her father a lot – to share with Benjamin, who would just grind the paintbrush into the pads of colour, ruining them.

In her father's opinion it was essential that she kept her desk neat, but Elizabeth had seen his desk at the surgery and had seen Miss Loveling's desk at her two-storey house overlooking the bay in Hobart. Elizabeth knew an element of haphazardness had to be introduced if she were to be an artist. Elizabeth needed a purpose. She needed an adventure. All around her were people with both.

Val

Val heard a clunk from her daughter's room; it was hard to believe Elizabeth was tidying, but there you were.

Val headed upstairs, took the new dress from the hook on her bedroom door and slid it off its hanger. She ran her hand down its length. She was a sharp and quick dressmaker and stitched her name into everything she sewed. This one from a McCall's, a pickle-green fabric with tiny spots. Val sang as she stepped into it, zipped herself up, clipped on earrings. She tipped her head forward and spritzed perfume onto the back of her neck like her mother used to do. She hoped the children would play a game or put on a dance or a show in the lounge room for her and Pam, who had known and loved Elizabeth and Benjamin since they were born, calling them her pair of socks.

It had been Val's idea, the invitation for Pam to drive up from Hobart. Pam had written in July to say she was starting a new children's picture book, this time about a zoo and what happened when the animals were alone at night. In August, Pam wrote to say the project was going swimmingly. In September, she wrote that she was stuck and would never write another book as long as she lived. She couldn't get the three child characters *right*, or even close to right. The illustrations, she said, were as frightful as figures on a biscuit tin. Any chance Val's children would model for her? Pam had rescued Val many times, and she'd recently been of great comfort following the news of Gordon's illness.

It was settled then, Val wrote to her, which was a fun thing to say. Pam would come and stay the night, or two, or three, if she wished. Val would put her in the spare room upstairs with the view of the plum trees. She would make sure her own children and a friend of Elizabeth's would be available to pose. She didn't know much about drawing but she knew plenty about children doing what they were told. She promised Pam hot meals and good gossip, bottles of wine or beer. She would make sure the children weren't grumpy and their faces were clean.

Val opened her compact and powdered her cheeks, picturing her smart friend. Pam Loveling was unusual and had to be studied to be understood. No good would come of trying to comprehend her for a few minutes at a time. She lived with her friend Colleen, a woman with deep brown eyes and black hair, who played tennis and taught music and fixed instruments for a living. Pam went through periods of having lots of money to being skint, although she'd never once asked Val for help in that respect. The idea of a job at a school or library or in a firm of some sort seemed distasteful to Pam. She and Colleen had moved house several times together and had holidayed in Melbourne and Cairns, Singapore and Cape Town. Recently, Pam sent the children a postcard from St Kilda Beach, saying she and Colleen were having a wonderful time eating all the ice cream they could get their hands on.

ELIZABETH

Her mother caught her on the landing as they both came out of their bedrooms. She had pins between her lips, and her arms were raised behind her head, pushing and patting her hair. 'There,' she said and beamed.

'You look pretty,' Elizabeth said, glad she'd found the yellow-striped skirt her mother had sewn for her.

Her mother put her arms out like a dancer and did a half-twirl in both directions. One hand held money and a scrap of paper. 'Here's the list. Thank you, darling El. Quick as you can.'

cream

cornflour

cigarettes

tin of peaches

lollies for Pam

Elizabeth walked down Elphin Road towards the milk bar that was run by Mr Driscoll, who believed the world was going to end soon. That's why he ate loads of chips and chocolates from his own shop, he said.

Inside, Elizabeth selected the items from her mother's shopping list and bundled them into her arms. She asked Mr Driscoll for her father's brand of cigarettes since she didn't know Miss Loveling's. He showed her the newspaper he was reading; on the page a story about Kennedy and nuclear testing. Mr Driscoll's half head of hair was always messy, his expression always sleepy, hands grimy with chip salt. No point denying yourself treats if the Russians were tinkering with the whole place anyway.

President Kennedy said there would be an American man on the moon by the end of the decade, beating the Soviets, getting there first. Winning was important to JFK, and that part Elizabeth understood. At school, when she'd asked Miss Stein in science about the chances of an Australian man reaching the moon, her teacher agreed that she didn't think it was likely. Then Heather Price had said, 'Maybe one day we'll be *living* on the moon,' and Elizabeth had waited for Miss Stein's reaction before she made up her mind.

Mr Driscoll kept his eyes on his newspaper while placing the tin and packets and the bottle of cream into a bag.

'I know a secret,' Elizabeth said. 'About my uncle.'

Mr Driscoll paused. His tongue was out, pressed against his thumb, ready to turn the page. 'You know a what?'

'Actually, I know two secrets. One is about me.'

He took his thumb from his mouth, looking baffled. 'Well, that seems fine, yes? Secrets about yourself?'

'And my uncle.'

'The one about you is probably the one to concern yourself with.'

'Yes, okay.' Elizabeth gathered the handles of the bag.

'You want your change? Here.'

She watched Mr Driscoll help himself to a sherbet stick from a glass cylinder. He folded his newspaper into a tight half and carried on reading it, nibbling on the lolly, as she backed out to leave.

She'd have to hurry or she'd miss Wendy's arrival at the house. Ten minutes and her friend would be there, and then they could fill Elizabeth's room with the burr of their secrets. Elizabeth turned over in her mind the important news she had for her mother, who could be relied on to tell her father when he got home from work. She imagined her parents made fevered and short-tempered by the news. When Elizabeth thought of being responsible for an argument like that, an orb of pleasure waxed in her chest.

Letting herself in the front gate, Elizabeth spied Wendy in her butterfly-print dress, a jumper round her waist and her hair in plaits, astride her bicycle, edging up the driveway.

Elizabeth decided to tell her straight away. She piloted Wendy over to the grass, where she sat her down, dropped her bike, then the bag, then flopped down onto her back. 'Guess what? I'm going to be an artist.'

Wendy's reaction, which was to seek out a scab on her ankle, was disappointing. Perhaps the sound of a bus or a barking dog had made her hard to hear. Elizabeth laid a hand on Wendy's arm. 'An *artist*. That's what I'll be when I grow up.'

'I thought you were going to be a scientist.'

Elizabeth scoffed – although she had to bung that on a bit. There was something so clanging, so jointed and silvery, about the word *scientist*. How good of Wendy to remember, though. This secret only worked if her best friend (devoted, funny, pretty too, if a little horsey) remembered what her previous dream had been. Only if Wendy recognised the polarity of the two occupations. Elizabeth knew one of each: her father, a doctor at a surgery on Hopkins Street, was a sort of scientist. He'd studied medicine, including the slicing open of people's bodies. And her mother's best friend, Miss Loveling, illustrated books for children. People knew her in Melbourne and even Sydney.

'Can you imagine spending all day, every day, drawing?' Elizabeth asked, sitting up. Through the bag, she rolled the bottle of cream back and forth on the grass. 'I could fly overseas and meet lots of people at galleries and shows.'

'What would you draw?' Wendy asked.

'Plants and flowers, I suppose. Landscapes. The insides of things. The sky.' Elizabeth thought of her uncle, now a pilot, and all those hours he would get to spend up in the clouds.

She had books to go on, examples to use till she got better, like the intricate four-by-four-inch illustrations in *Malady*. Elizabeth set herself evenings with the book on her lap and sheets of paper to copy images: the cabbage-like human heart, the set of lungs spread open like a butterfly, the weight and flex of an elbow joint. She hoped to get through at least a dozen and perhaps have the drawings bound into her own secret book to present to her parents, casually, over lunch one day. Maybe her father would offer to buy the set and frame them for his surgery. But, in the words of her uncle, she was getting ahead of herself. Coming from Gordon – kind but with only a vague interest in his niece and nephew, his face handsome and open, his wide-set clear blue eyes never quite resting on anyone – it was a fun thing to hear. When she said it to herself, it had a harder edge. Yes, of course her father would have bought a cute scribble or two when she was younger. But she was almost fourteen. The drawings would have to be good to mean anything.

She felt despair pulling at her, and for a few seconds she couldn't think of anything good. 'We'd better take the groceries in to Mum,' she said. 'Then we can go upstairs.'

VAL

In the kitchen was a storeroom under the stairs. Val took down her apron from inside the door, looped it over her head and tied it behind her waist. She caught the rapid chatter, the sound of shoes on stones, as Elizabeth and Wendy came up the path to the front door.

'You're here,' she said, and the girls came through to the kitchen.

Val blew a strand of hair off her forehead. She touched her daughter's friend on the hand. 'Wendy, how are you? What's been the best part of your day?'

Wendy shrugged. 'Nothing's happened till now. This is the best part.' She was a thin girl with an upturned nose and a patter of dark-brown birthmarks down one side of her neck. She beamed. 'Thanks for having me.'

Elizabeth undid the handles of the bag and unpacked the groceries onto the kitchen table.

'Benjamin?' Val called. 'I need to see you before Miss Loveling gets here.'

Footsteps down the stairs, the thrum of an object shuddering along the balustrades and then Benjamin came into the kitchen. He was nine years old with thick black hair he asked his mother to keep cut short. He was tall for his age. He kept his room clean and never answered back. He submitted to baths and helped his father by running out for cigarettes and lawn mower fuel. A beautiful boy, a good boy. Benjamin, like Gordon, was so obedient it was almost irritating – but imagine complaining about a son who did absolutely everything he was told. Underneath it all, Val sensed reservation, solitude, even resentment. As he grew older, Val hoped, her boy might open up. Her husband, Stuart, didn't think it was healthy for children to be so serious.

'Now, Benjamin, Wendy here has been invited around for tea. Do you mind? The only lad in the house?'

He shook his head solemnly.

'Uncle Gordon will be thrilled to know we're looking up at him tonight, admiring his plane and how beautifully he's learnt to fly.'

'Will Miss Loveling be here for it?' Wendy asked.

'Very much so. She'll be delighted by it.'

'It isn't for hours, though,' Benjamin said.

Val clapped her hands. 'I know what we'll do – a prize! How about you children all draw a picture for Miss Loveling? Whatever you'd like. And when she gets here, she can be the judge.' She patted the pockets of her apron and pulled out a comb and a milk bottle top. She slipped them back inside. 'I'll find something terrific to be the prize. Elizabeth, you can get paper and pencils. I'd best stay in the kitchen with the lamb.'

'What if we're not any good at drawing?' Benjamin asked.

'Well,' Elizabeth said, 'I guess you won't win then, will you? Miss Loveling is very famous and talented.'

Val clasped Benjamin's head to her belly and gave him a kiss. 'There's nothing wrong with trying to impress someone. Much to be said for it.'

Elizabeth started up the stairs with Wendy and Benjamin following, and Val turned towards the kitchen. She had the potatoes left to do; peel them under the tap and let them sit in a bowl of cold water with a tablespoon of vinegar – a rare, clever thing her mother-in-law taught her when she and Stuart were first married. She could hear the children above as she stood at the sink. Their talk and fuss rising and falling like a passing car outside, or an aeroplane overhead.

ELIZABETH

Uncle Gordon would land the aeroplane at the airstrip a few miles away, where he'd taken his flying lessons and earnt his licence. The route he'd planned would take him over Newstead at half past eight that night. That's about as much as Elizabeth knew. In winter, Gordon had been diagnosed with an illness. Something very adult, with many syllables, oddly metallic-sounding, and she had tried on three separate occasions, pen in hand, to wheedle the word from her mother so she could find it in *Malady*. But her mother wouldn't repeat it. 'And you mustn't ask him either, if that's what you were thinking,' her mother had said. 'That's like poison.'

VAL

'That's like poison,' Val had told her daughter, 'doing that to someone.'

And Elizabeth had done something unexpected then, reaching forward to put her arms around her mother's neck, lowering her onto the couch – the way a lover would, Val was alarmed to think. Elizabeth had shifted into her mother's lap, and Val had been telescoped back in time to the sensation of her daughter's body when she was soft and small and unable to sit still for five seconds. Val rubbed circles across her back.

'Uncle Gordon won't die,' Elizabeth said.

Then it came to Val how much she used to pretend with her daughter. Pretend to gobble at Elizabeth's fat, fudgy arms, saying, *Is there gold in this tree trunk? Is there honey? Any nectar?* The girl in hysterics, her hands messing about in Val's hair, begging her to stop, saying, *There's no gold! No honey!* These sweet things Val remembered – she hoped her children would, too. But would they remember the other times? Things she would never admit to a minister, let alone an illustrator of books for children. An illustrator who'd never had kids and could not really understand, no matter how many times she visited or sent postcards or offered to have them stay at her house, how *difficult* it had been to care for two small children almost entirely on her own. Quite easily, she could convince herself that of course they recalled, could feel, residually, her hot breath on their faces. The violence of *I hate you* on the soft spot between their shoulder blades.

The sound of a car turning into the driveway. Dear Pam. Val reached for her lipstick in the dish above the servery, uncapped it and bent into her reflection in a saucepan. She hoped the children wouldn't come thundering down the stairs with their assortment of tearaway enthusiasm and needy questions. Give the two of them a minute alone. Supposing, Val thought with a moment of panic, Pam had brought Colleen. Meeting Colleen at a party for one of Pam's books had done nothing to smooth Val's feeling of unease. Colleen was a nice woman who looked at home among Pam's bookish friends. Val watched her – petite in a cream jacket and skirt – move from group to group and touch the arms of men and women she was speaking to, laughing. Colleen reminded Val of a fox terrier, fearless and alert. Val felt a pricking behind her eyes.

She would think about this later. Would remember these flashes of irritation and wonder why they kept returning to her year after year.

Val walked out to the driveway and saw just the one figure, in the driver's seat. Relief. She breathed out and knocked on her friend's window. 'Pammy, dear. You made it.'

Pam wound down the window. 'Oh, it's good to see you, Val.'

Still only the lightest dusting of powder across her cheeks and nose and no lipstick at all; Pam had never liked the stuff. Her brown hair was in a low bun, her fringe thick across her forehead. Val reached in, trembling but strong with her grip, and grabbed her hand. Val was drinking this in: the pinprick of anticipation, the start of the evening before the children were tired and hungry and demanding things from her, the anticipation of watching her brother sail through the sky. Almost everyone who was going to be here had arrived. The food was cooling or warming as it needed to be. No-one needed to go anywhere. Stuart had told her he would try to make it home for the aeroplane, and Val trusted that, yes, he would be on time.

She carried Pam's suitcase up the front path. Inside, she set it beside the stairs. She admired Pam's earrings and her tobacco-coloured coat.

'Where are they, then?' Pam asked. She pulled off her coat and stuffed her gloves into her handbag. 'Your sausages? The two divine parrots? The steak and kidney pies?'

'Upstairs,' Val said, 'trying to impress you with their drawings.'

'Well, that *is* sweet.'

'I have a surprise for you. It's about Gordon.'

'Oh?' Pam undid a shopping bag and pulled out two packets of chocolate creams, a cool bottle of wine and a white box from a bakery. She reached across the kitchen table and set the biscuits on top of each other. 'Is he all right?'

Val had told Pam in one of her letters that there had been a diagnosis. But Val found it difficult, even on paper, to say it, so she hadn't. She set her shoulders back, smiling. 'You will see him tonight.'

'For tea?'

'In his aeroplane.'

Pam raised an eyebrow. 'In the sky?'

Yes, in the sky. But Val wasn't about to convey how excited she was. Not after the raised eyebrow. Four years younger than Val and Pam, Gordon used to trail behind them, doing the girls' bidding, fixing their bicycle tyres, helping them hide and care for the puppy they'd found wandering the park. All up, the whole adventure had probably lasted only a day, but deciding what the dog should eat and where to get a blanket that wouldn't be missed: they'd been in that together. They'd known one another for so long. *In the sky?* Yes, in the sky.

Val turned away. In any case there were the potatoes. And drinks for them both. She poured lemonade into two short glasses that they clinked together.

'Oh, this is going to be fun,' Pam said.

Val fished a cube of ice out of her glass and popped it in her mouth.

ELIZABETH

Here is Elizabeth, six years old, crouched beside the pond in her backyard. She wears a lemon-coloured band in her blonde hair and a white smocked dress that her mother bought from a lady at church. In Elizabeth's hands are two frogs that she's been gazing at for several minutes. Before they were frogs they were tadpoles. Before they were tadpoles they were eggs, but not like hen's eggs. *Picture a tiny bubble*, her mother explained, before Elizabeth had seen a tadpole for real. She had marvelled at their jumpiness, their brown bodies wriggling down, down, down like something swallowed but not chewed.

Her mother has warned her not to get her dress dirty; she is taking Elizabeth and her baby brother to a magic show at the school, once Benjamin has woken from his sleep. Elizabeth would love the magician to multiply her brother. A tap of a wand on his soft, perfect nose, and three or four more infants would pop out like a string of paper dolls. She adores Benjamin. She loves when she is permitted to hold him, which is often. *His neck, watch his neck,* the adults around her say. She always cups his head gently.

Elizabeth lowers her hand to the edge of the pond and dips her fingers beneath the surface of the water. The frogs' tiny legs kick at her skin. They hop off into the muck.

At the magic show there are rows of chairs dragged out from a nearby classroom. Babies in prams squint in the glare while their mothers linger at the cake stall. Tables covered in things for sale have been arranged like points on a clock with the stage marking twelve, at the top. And on the stage, a sign covered in stars and the name 'Charlie Charm' is strung between two hooks. Children run across the sun-bathed, balloon-dotted oval.

Has there ever been such an exciting day as this?

The magic, Elizabeth tells her father when she gets home and her mother is lowering Benjamin into a bath, was *real*. It was all real. The rabbit that the magician drew out of his hat was white with pink in its ears and until that moment she hadn't known that rabbits had pink in their ears. Her father makes a show of turning Elizabeth's head to one side – 'Now, wait a minute' – proclaiming that her ears are pink, too, and does that make her a rabbit? Elizabeth giggles, loving her father extravagantly when he's like this. No. She is no more a rabbit than a frog.

'What else did he do?' her father asks, his face close to hers, his fingers on the band in her hair. 'The magician?'

Tricks with cards. A large silver coin that he showed them from the stage, circled between his fingers before disappearing then reappearing under someone's chair. One trick where his glove ended up in the lap of another, luckier, girl. With his wand, Charlie Charm tapped a balloon and it popped and the adults laughed. But then he tapped it a second time and it swelled up and was whole again. Elizabeth heard the rush of the adults' breath, and the children's breath around her. She saw her own mother's face, open with sunny surprise. But Elizabeth had guessed what would happen to the balloon. *She* had known it.

VAL

It would be a wonderful evening, full of magic. Val took out her favourite dish, the one shaped like a lettuce leaf. She shook the paper bag of lollies into it, popped a cobber in her mouth. Pam had a sweet tooth, said lollies helped her draw.

'Want one?' Val asked, turning to her friend, who plucked three or four out and arranged them in her palm.

'I love your frock,' Pam said. 'Such talent. I bet you made it in an hour.'

'Not too far off, actually,' Val said, winking.

'I'm amazed but not surprised. What can I help with?' she asked.

'Nothing at all,' Val said.

The cooking smells cheered the room. The warmth from the oven dulled Val's fluctuation between excitement and fear. She poured another drink, this time the wine Pam had brought. When Gordon got sick Stuart had told her, 'Whatever happens, things will work out fine.' Val guessed that being calm and logical were useful traits for a doctor who was often called upon to assess smashed elbows after motorcycle accidents, the sticky infected eyes of children, heart murmurs that kept his old patients awake. What Stuart likely meant, what he likely believed, was this: no matter what happened around them, their own family would remain intact. Mother, father, daughter, son – they were a constant. They deserved robust and unbroken lifespans, so that's what they would get.

Val, who was often seized with palpable images of the ways Elizabeth and Benjamin might die, wanted very much to have Stuart's confidence. But her children could be hit by a car taking a corner too close to the kerb. They could drown in the sea. She and Stuart might wake one morning to find a white ladder up against the side of the house leading to a child's bedroom. Scarlet fever, mumps, measles. She collected possible disasters like she collected sewing patterns. But Stuart existed methodically. He shrank his worries down to the size of a single pea while hers flourished through her body like tumours.

Val hadn't asked about Colleen yet. 'I'm sorry,' Val said. 'How's Colleen?'

'She's well, thank you.'

'Well, next time you come,' Val said breezily, 'you'll have to bring her. No point in her being alone down there, is there?'

Pam stilled. She smiled. 'That would be lovely.' She reached across and patted Val's hand.

Val collected the wineglasses and jerked her head towards the lounge room. 'Let's drink in here.'

ELIZABETH

On the path running down one side of the house, Elizabeth and Wendy perched on an upturned wheelbarrow outside the low window. Inside, her mother and Miss Loveling had gathered in the lounge room before tea. Wendy cupped her chin in her hand, trying to appear more interested than Elizabeth knew she was. So far nothing much exciting had happened. Her mother sat barefoot on the couch. She had reapplied her lipstick. Elizabeth hadn't asked, but the answer would be no. No lipstick till she was a thousand years old.

Miss Loveling shifted in her red cardigan. She reached for her glass and finished it in one gulp. This made the women giggle, which seemed to intrigue Wendy for a moment.

'What happened?' she whispered.

'Nothing.'

'Ooh, mind the bottom of that,' Elizabeth heard her mother say, after the giggling had stopped. 'On the armrest, yes, that's right.'

They watched Elizabeth's mother pluck at a magazine, flicking the paper swiftly, her voice lowered towards the pages. She said something about stains on suede, and cornflour. Something about sore feet and needing them rubbed.

'We'll put some on a plate with the olives. The children won't touch them,' Elizabeth heard her mother say.

Miss Loveling said, 'Kitchen?' and her mother nodded.

Through the window, Elizabeth watched Miss Loveling stand. She pulled her mother to her feet and they carried their glasses away.

That was it? That's what adults talked about when they were alone? Foot rubs and olives bought from the Greeks on the corner and the marks left by glasses on a suede couch? So *boring*. Elizabeth could imagine fifty more interesting things to talk about, right now, off the top of her head. Adults were so unfocused, so likely to bring up old news just to start new conversations. And they spent their money on boring things: repairs to appliances and second pairs of the same shoes. Elizabeth would never say, of course. No-one ever asked her, of course. She had better things in mind for her secret stash of notes counted nightly and tucked into a lolly jar from Paris.

If you could stow enough of yourself away, there was more of you in the world, not less.

VAL

Val had been seven when Charles Lindbergh flew in an unbroken arc from New York to Paris. Newspapers showed his aeroplane and his warm, handsome face. She'd been only slightly younger than Benjamin was now – but it had been such a different time. Things had felt nimble and light.

Val had impressed upon Stuart how important it was for him to see Gordon fly the plane alone, for the first time. She lifted out six plates, setting one to the side for Stuart. She would serve his and cover it with foil to keep warm in the oven.

She watched Pam pull a cloth pencil case and black sketchbook out of her suitcase. 'It's the zoo book I need your children for,' she told Val, rummaging for something else. 'I can't shake the idea, haven't for years, so I figured I'd better write it so it can leave me alone.'

'Does that happen often?'

'Colleen calls them ghost ideas.' Pam straightened, slipping lollies into her pocket.

'I can't imagine how your mind works.' Val fingered the sleeve of her new green dress. Producing things like the spotty frock would have to be enough for her. 'It's a marvellous idea.'

'If I ever finish it.'

'You will. You have it in your sights now.'

They had been the two smallest girls in school from day one. Val, timid and sensory and interested in everything; Pam, creative and commanding and absolutely everyone's favourite. Val had loved her for this. Now she saw in her own daughter a need to be liked, to be seen and validated. To know more and to solve problems. A thirst like hers would be an assault on the world. *Do less*, Val would think when she watched Elizabeth skip from project to project. *Be invisible, even occasionally. Make* that *your goal*. But this was deeply unpopular nowadays, and she was glad she'd never told Pam or Stuart. What if Amelia Earhart had remained invisible? Hadn't that woman made the world a more interesting place in the long stretch of time since Val was a girl?

Over the years, Val had felt her body thicken with age, grow a little more with each pregnancy. There had been a third baby and that had been hard to recover from. Half her body didn't know what the other half had endured and so it kept thrumming along as though the baby was near her, and her breasts were flame-hot, and it was hard for the weight to come off. One nurse told her of women who lived in the bush who never got to stay a single night in the hospital with their sick newborns. This memory – of folding socks and cutting sandwiches for Elizabeth and Benjamin while she waited for news from the hospital – squeezed her very hard. It probably would for the rest of her life.

'Bring those,' Val said, nodding to the sketchbook and pencil case. 'Quick – first I'll show you the new bedspread and the bowl Benjamin made me in Sunday school.'

They wandered up to Val and Stuart's bedroom. The house was quiet in the late afternoon. Sunlight fell across the silky-oak dressing table, the wardrobe, the matching valet where Stuart kept his cufflinks and comb. On the wall hung their wedding photo. Pam had been Val's bridesmaid in lilac silk and gloves, with orchids that almost touched the ground. On Val's face in the photograph was the quiet confidence and polish of being young, of being garlanded in flowers, wrapped in organza.

The cream carpet was plush underneath their shoes, and Val sidestepped the creak in the floor at the end of her bed. She ran a hand over the bedspread stitched across in a diamond pattern. Her sleeping had not improved since it arrived.

At the dressing table, Pam asked, 'Is this the bowl?'

Val nodded. 'Turn it over.'

Pam read: '*Mum. All my love. B.*' She let out a laugh. 'Where did he get that from? That's exquisite.'

'I suspect it was what they all had to write. But it's sweet.'

'I hated Sunday school.'

'Did you?' Val was utterly surprised. 'I loved it. What else was there to do? All those old people chattering away at you, slipping you barley sugars.'

'I never could sit still. I hated being told to.'

'And we had those baskets with our coins inside.'

'You did love that basket.'

Talking like this was nice, on the edge of old times. Val was glad Pam would be staying at least one night and hoped it would be longer. Her heart swelled at the beautiful evening ahead with the children and the plane going by. She sat at the end of the bed.

'Does that feel like a long time ago to you?' Val asked. 'It feels like an age to me.'

Pam seemed to think about the question seriously. 'Actually, could be yesterday for all I know.'

'Huh. How strange.' Val lay back on the bed and loosened her shoes until they dropped to the floor. 'I'll just be a minute,' she said and laughed.

Pam lay beside her, and they breathed in time. Val had been awake since four in the morning, no good reason. She relished the sweetness of being horizontal and silent on her soft bed. She closed her eyes and was aware of the scents in her bedroom in the way Pam might be experiencing them. On the bedside table she kept a silver-lidded tin filled with a scoop of potpourri, and lavender in muslin sachets in the top drawers. Other smells mingled: Stuart's talcum powder, and the fresh sunny scent of the newly laundered bedspread. The lamb must be almost ready because its richness was there too, wafting upstairs.

Pam drew a sharp breath. 'Colleen's mother passed away.'

Val turned, and saw Pam was trying not to cry. 'What? When?'

'A month ago.'

'Oh, the pet. How is she?'

Pam lifted her hand from her thigh and tilted it. *So-so.*

'When was the funeral?' Val asked. 'I would have come.' The contest inside. Shame at the lie but unable to admit it.

Pam shook her head. 'Neither of us went. They hadn't seen each other in fifteen years.'

'What did she – in the end?'

'Cancer.'

Val exhaled deeply. She gripped the bedspread with both hands.

'Colleen, well, she doesn't even know what … which …' Pam moved her hands over her torso. 'Her sisters won't talk to her.'

Val felt squeezed all over again. 'I'd best check on the tea.' She rolled onto her side and pushed herself up. She looked down at Pam and touched her shoulder. 'Unless you want me to stay. Unless we say hang it and the kids can eat porridge.'

'Let them,' Pam said, reaching for Val and sounding at once as old and as young as Val had ever known. 'One minute? Lie down.'

Val would never get over the fear of losing her brother, who might very well survive, Stuart had said, in his matter-of-fact way.

Who knew? They would all do what they could. She saw in her children the relationship she and Gordon had. A relationship with cracks and crevices. Ignoring each other, summoning help, picking fights, until one day it was easy to convince the other that your love was the same, even after years of pieces being taken out of you. Until one day your brother knocked on your door in Newstead and said with a winged smile that he was going to learn to fly, that he'd always wanted to, and although it was a small thing it was a skill he would like to know. She'd scoffed at that: *a small thing*. Imagine the man who thinks enormous things are small. *Her brother would learn to fly.* She felt tears coming.

Colleen's sisters must be unfeeling or wicked, or both.

Pam echoed Val's thought. 'Such unkind sisters and daughters.'

How on earth Val was the mother of a girl, a thirteen-year-old, she couldn't quite fathom.

But she'd have to stop this moping. Downstairs and all around her things needed to get done. She said to Pam, 'Why don't you go see what the children are up to? Send them straight to me if they muck around.'

ELIZABETH

For the art prize they were in Elizabeth's bedroom. She stood with her back against the door, holding a notepad and coloured pencils in a box. Wendy sat cross-legged on the bed, and Benjamin was prattling on beside his sister's duchess, touching all the objects that were usually forbidden, like the photograph of Elizabeth, their mum and Gordon at Sandy Bay, and half a paper wheel of circle stickers, and novelty beer coasters bound in string, and a bottle of red nail polish she'd tried once and was now dried up.

'Benjamin, are your hands clean?'

Elizabeth could see that the prospects of a roast and his Uncle Gordon as a pilot, staying up late and being permitted in the yard after dark were fuelling Benjamin's excitement. 'If you don't want your dessert, later, Lizzie,' he said, 'will you give it to me?'

She made a face at her brother, who was lovable but predictable in his greediness. 'If I don't want it, which I *will*, I'll give it to Wendy.'

Benjamin made a face back. 'Fine.' He wiped his nose on his sleeve. 'I think we should play a game.'

'What game?' Wendy asked. 'We've got to draw.'

'No, that's boring. This is a game I've made up,' he said, although most likely he hadn't. Not yet. 'It's called Airman and it's just like … charades.'

'Charades are boring,' Elizabeth said.

'The *game,*' he repeated, 'is called Airman.'

Elizabeth thrust a sheet of paper towards him. 'Everyone has to draw a picture to see who's the best.'

Benjamin lifted a tin off her duchess and stubbed open the lid with his thumbnail. Unusually for him, he was keyed up and mischievous. 'I don't want to.'

Wendy was friendly about it all. Sitting forward, she said, 'Do what Lizzie says or you won't get to see the aeroplane.' Benjamin screwed up his face, almost certainly thinking hard and unable to follow the lines of logic back to the spot where Wendy had control over whether he walked outside in a few hours and what, precisely, he would see.

He shook his head, darkly, and picked up a pencil.

'Why don't you draw an iguana, Benjamin?' Wendy said.

'Or a tapeworm,' Elizabeth added, pretending to sketch.

'Leave me alone,' he said.

Elizabeth, while wanting to demonstrate to her mother that art couldn't be summoned on demand and shouldn't be ranked, also wanted, desperately, to win the prize. She was confident it would end up being money from their mother's purse rather than the milk bottle top or the comb, and she could do with a boost to her funds in the lolly jar. She could do with reminding everyone of the talented recesses that existed in her brain. All the better to show how she'd been able to cultivate these with almost no help from the adults in her life. Her talent would emerge in a way that seemed miraculous.

There was a knock at the door and Benjamin jumped up, without having made a single stroke on his paper, to let Miss Loveling in. He stood with his hands behind his back and allowed her to kiss him. She slipped a hand into a pocket of her skirt and tossed three Minties onto the bed.

'Finally,' Benjamin said, lunging for them. 'Thanks.'

'I bought lollies for you too,' Elizabeth said.

Miss Loveling was taller than their mother and thinner. Her hair was greyer now and longer than was the style. Elizabeth admired how her mother read the *Women's Weekly* and made adjustments to her hair every few months. Miss Loveling seemed more inclined to do her own thing. And she didn't crowd Elizabeth and Benjamin with loads of questions about their teachers and what they'd learnt at school. She was Benjamin's godmother, which, to Elizabeth, seemed a mistake and probably not one anybody could ever politely reverse. Elizabeth was much better suited to being the goddaughter of a famous illustrator of children's books. Once Benjamin had even called Miss Loveling's friend 'Gail' instead of Colleen.

Wendy had met Elizabeth's sort-of aunty before, had received compliments on her dress and questions about tennis, and a comment about her birthmarks, which she didn't seem to mind.

'Sit on the bed with us,' Wendy invited now.

'I'll set myself up over here, I think,' Miss Loveling said. She motioned to the writing desk and chair beneath the window. 'I'm getting old.'

'I can't wait to get old,' Wendy said.

'Well, *older*. Not *old*,' Elizabeth corrected.

'There's a difference,' Wendy told Miss Loveling.

'Of course,' she replied. She picked up a pen, the blue one with an orange cap, and started making short sharp lines as though she was relieving the paper of an itch.

Wendy returned to her drawing: long slices like the segments of an orange. Elizabeth leaned in. A hot air balloon. She turned to Miss Loveling. 'Do you think I could go to university one day?'

'Absolutely. Why not?'

The magic of those words while Wendy nodded beside her, looking up from her picture. Elizabeth caught her smile.

'I have three brothers and two sisters,' Wendy told Miss Loveling. 'My oldest sister, Jackie, is about to become a teacher and what if she gets a job at our school and becomes *my* teacher? Can you imagine?'

Miss Loveling blanched. 'That sounds horrible. I should write a book about that.'

For some time, Elizabeth had been watching her sketch a boy in knee-high socks and two girls in chequered school dresses. Elizabeth thought Miss Loveling knew more than most people about the human body. Her brother's expressions were right there on the page, in the face of the boy. Elizabeth was beginning to perceive a gulf between her work and Miss Loveling's. By now, she had discarded her drawing of a pair of hands and was working on a stem of kangaroo paw.

'Did you always want to be an artist?'

Miss Loveling nodded, and Elizabeth checked to see that Wendy had seen.

'Why do you like it?'

Miss Loveling tilted her chin to the ceiling, and her face softened. 'You can draw something and remember it forever,' she said. 'Plus it's fun and I'm terrific at it.'

The girls grinned. Pride like this was not encouraged. It was a shock to hear a grown-up say it aloud.

Elizabeth asked, 'What's your book about?'

'It's about animals in a zoo and what they get up to when the caretakers lock up for the night.'

'What are your characters called?'

'Haven't decided. Certainly not Elizabeth, Benjamin and Wendy.' Miss Loveling jabbed the air near Benjamin with her pen. 'That would spoil the secret.'

'Where's the zoo?' Benjamin asked, colouring.

'Not sure. Maybe nowhere precisely. There used to be a zoo in Hobart. It had polar bears, did you know that?'

'I know it had Tasmanian tigers.' He looked up. 'But they're all dead now.'

'That's what they think. They also kept lions.'

Benjamin said, 'I wish they had lions there now.'

'Do you? I think it would be a frightening place to live if you were a lion.'

'Why?'

'Because it isn't in their nature to be locked up. They might not live as long.'

'Have you ever seen a real lion, in real life?' Elizabeth asked. 'Has Colleen?'

Miss Loveling nodded but said nothing more about it.

'What are you doing now?' Wendy got up and stood beside Miss Loveling, placing a hand on her shoulder.

'I'm looking for traces of my characters in you, and traces of you in my characters. I'll need to make them … ooh, a bit less hearty. Their hair wouldn't have shone this much.'

'Why?' Elizabeth asked.

'There was hunger. Even here, in Tasmania, in the thirties, when your mother and I were at school and there were lions and polar bears at the zoo.' She put down her pen. 'Now. Who's ready for judging? Do we have a prize?'

'Benjamin, go check,' Elizabeth ordered. She needed one more minute with her artwork.

Her brother abandoned his drawing, crushing it with his palm as he stood. He trotted downstairs. It was almost silent in the bedroom. They listened to Benjamin's voice in the kitchen, her mother's low and absent-minded *hmmm*. Elizabeth sharpened her red pencil one last time. She pictured her mother unhooking her handbag from the hat rack in the hall and digging through, unzipping her purse. Elizabeth heard glee in her brother's voice. She imagined her mother's face flushed from the heat of the oven.

Miss Loveling stood and moved to the doorway. 'Val? Come up for the judging.'

Two sets of feet on the stairs, then, and Elizabeth waited to see what they'd return with. Benjamin entered the room with a ten-shilling note stuck to his forehead, his hands held up high in case it fell.

'Wow,' Wendy said.

'It's ten,' Benjamin said, lifting it off his skin. 'Ten!'

'All right, Benjamin.' Their mother smiled at the attention. 'The competition was my idea so I thought I'd better come up with a good prize.'

Elizabeth wondered how much her mother knew about her secret jar from Paris stuffed with money.

Miss Loveling took the three drawings and laid them out across Elizabeth's bed: Wendy's hot air balloon floating over a vast yet unfinished green valley, Benjamin's circus tent surrounded by animal performers, and Elizabeth's scarlet-fingered kangaroo paw. For a moment Elizabeth thought Miss Loveling would decline to choose a winner, on the basis that they were children and therefore deserved special treatment. Or, worse, give the prize to Benjamin for no reason other than being the youngest.

'Elizabeth, it's definitely you.' Miss Loveling turned to Benjamin and Wendy. 'She's done the best drawing and she deserves to win.'

They clapped dutifully and abandoned their own drawings on the bed, their interest in them now lost.

'May I?' Her mother held out her hand to Miss Loveling, eyeing Elizabeth for permission. The countless drawings they had shared since Elizabeth was a toddler. 'Oh, darling.'

'Quite the artist,' Miss Loveling said, and returned to her own sketchbook. Her gaze flickered between Benjamin and the paper in front. Elizabeth saw countless Benjamins in all manner of poses and expressions: crouching (perhaps at a fountain); peering (perhaps through steel bars); arms thrown into the air; pointing; laughing; sulking. One in which his mouth was a dark circle of excitement.

'She is indeed,' her mother said. 'Did you know, Pam, that El could draw faces – real, identifiable faces – by the time she was two, two and a half?' Elizabeth liked this. She'd heard this story before. 'It's a gorgeous kangaroo paw, my dear. Ten shillings for you. Benjamin? To your sister, please.' Her mother kissed her, retied her apron and headed back downstairs.

VAL

Val ran a knife around the inside of the cake tin then turned the sponge out onto the wire rack, peeled away the paper and set it the right way up. With the raspberry jam it would be Pam's favourite. A custard bubbled on the stove. Save a slice of the cake for Gordon, and he and Pam could share it later tonight over coffee, or for morning tea tomorrow.

If Pam could just see Gordon stepping down from the aeroplane, unwrapping his scarf, his cheeks flushed from the exertion of being an aviator, she might fall in love with him. Gordon could be directed this way and that – he'd go along with being fallen in love with. Val even imagined it was the aeroplane making all the decisions, her brother blinking, sitting up, murmuring into the control panel, *Yes, whatever you think, over to you.* After almost forty years of acquiescence, perhaps Gordon's body had decided to get on with the business of making decisions and had even let a passing disease take hold.

She wished she'd known about Colleen's mother's death from a letter – the better to know what to say.

In the fridge she found the jam and dipped a spoon in and then into her mouth. She squinted through the window at the arrangement of native plums and swamp gums at the end of the garden. She stopped, the spoon on her tongue. Val would love nothing more than to catch Pam and her brother sharing cake at a table in the sun, or plucking at the leaves of a tree and smiling into each other's faces. Stranger things had happened after people grew up together and all that good-natured fighting and name-calling fell away. Maybe their childhood would prove to yield all sorts of love affairs.

ELIZABETH

All afternoon Elizabeth had fought off a strange tide of feeling about Uncle Gordon. The smooth white underbelly of the machine soaring from one side of the sky to the other would be magical to see. She both desperately wanted to see him in his aeroplane – maybe even a wave out the window – and desperately didn't. Unease slithered through her at the thought of the complicated, heavy machine and its contraptions. Her uncle was not a strong man. He was gentle and easily distracted. And he was sick.

Suddenly, Elizabeth decided she'd had enough of Wendy and needed a break. She looked out her window towards the garden and jumped off the bed.

'Wendy?' She told her to take Benjamin into the lounge room and watch the television, whatever they wanted, which of course did the trick, since Elizabeth's house was the only place Wendy got to watch any at all. And Benjamin was out of her bedroom like a shot, urging Wendy behind him, 'Come on, come on.'

In the backyard was the woodshed. Elizabeth had seen a whole family of spiders there once, scampering out from under a bucket like spilt ink. White cockatoos liked to perch on the gutter above the double wooden doors, rocking and swaying, lifting their claws and putting them down carefully.

A fortnight ago she had come out to unlock the doors for Gordon, who needed something from inside.

'Uncle Gordon,' she'd said before she could stop herself, 'are you sick?'

That's like poison, her mother had said.

'Only a bit, El. Lots of people get sick, I'm afraid.'

He cleared his throat, and she saw him not as a whole but as bits of a body, like the four-by-four-inch illustrations in *Malady*. His face was no longer his face but a cross-section, his skull an open-cut quarry. Ghoulish with its two rows of teeth alive and bared, the tongue a creature from the deep. Gordon had been wearing a blue jumper, and Elizabeth saw beneath it to his chest cavity: his heart the shape of a vegetable pulled from the soil. When he lifted his arm to cough: an exposed elbow joint. She saw the bones of his fingers and their hard eagerness to flicker and tap.

'Dad's a doctor.'

'So you know, then. About people getting sick.'

Elizabeth nodded.

'You're a smart girl. And there are many types of being sick, and not all of them – as good as your dad is – have easy cures.'

'What's it called?' she whispered. 'What's wrong with you?'

Uncle Gordon dropped his head.

It had been the wrong thing to say, she was sure. Anything else might have been better than that. Fear that began with her mother on the couch had grown, but wavered while she went to school and chatted with Wendy about hockey and tennis and whether there'd be a nuclear war soon. The fear was a fog around her head. *Uncle Gordon won't die*, is what she had told her mother and her mother had rubbed circles on her back.

Elizabeth could now see the tops of Wendy's and Benjamin's heads in the lounge room. Benjamin bobbed up and down on the couch. Elizabeth laid her hand on a tree. She should bring the washing in off the line for her mother. She looked at the pond. *Picture a tiny bubble*, her mother had said about the frogs.

Elizabeth's head felt untidy, not clear, not light.

One night last week she had dreamt of the aeroplane tumbling overhead. Out of the clouds it had appeared like a bird, Uncle Gordon a speck at the control panel. In that way of dreams, Elizabeth could feel his aliveness as though she was inside his chest cavity, and Gordon had been thinking about this moment for years, this part of himself that the aeroplane would prise open. The rhythm of the plane thrummed against the sky of her childhood – for the neighbourhood in her dream had slipped to the street she played in when she was younger.

She felt Gordon's grip on the yoke and the tightness across his chest and shoulders as the aeroplane soared. They were tilting and dipping while Launceston was a still and quiet town painted in fragments below. The mountains around them seemed to nod, perhaps something to scale up, up, up when Gordon grew with confidence. The river was dark beneath them, bearing boats like fish. Gordon coughed, and Elizabeth wondered if the cough was related to the name of the disease she didn't know. And then Gordon was saying something under his breath as the plane began to shudder.

What is it? she asked.

He seemed to shush her without saying a word.

What are you saying?

They breasted the air high above Tasmania. Suddenly Elizabeth could see all the way to the beach at Sandy Bay. The gulls were like crumbs on the sand, and she wondered why she and her uncle should be this close to the ground. Panic shook through her, and she saw the faces of her father and mother and baby Benjamin. A line of nausea drew itself across her throat. The ocean barrelled towards them, and the pines were tall and sharp.

At that moment, Gordon righted the machine. Elizabeth was

rocked, and her insides reassembled. She felt Gordon's relief, balmy and wide. But another feeling was lurking too. Pages of her beloved dictionary *Malady* seemed to flick before her until her mind rested, like a finger finding a word in a column, on 'despair'. A pair of emotions had propelled them. For a brief moment she had been on the edge of life but here was Elizabeth, firmly back within it. All was safe. Her uncle gave a wave from the window and slid the aeroplane out of view before she was woken by her mother: time for porridge and shoes and socks and school.

VAL

Val splashed gin into her glass, added ice and tonic and a thin slice of lemon. She held out a beer for Pam, who fixed herself a shandy without a pause in their conversation.

'The book isn't finished, Val. It's barely started.'

Val grabbed fistfuls of cutlery and motioned for Pam to follow her into the dining room. 'But that's why you're here. For the children to help you. Here – plate, please.'

'I felt so good about it. And now, nothing.'

'What about that treehouse one? With the magpies? Never thought you'd finish that, did you?'

Pam lowered herself into a chair, holding the plate aloft. She talked about her illustrations: her drawings were like spells she set out to cast, knowing what needed to go into each one, but where nothing was guaranteed. 'Sometimes they're bewitching. Other times they're a mess.'

'Oh, love.' Val felt like anything she said would be wrong. 'You'll get there.'

Pam put down the dinner plate and spun it. 'At some point I'll run out of oomph.'

'Never,' Val whispered.

'Or at least ideas.'

Val raised her voice. 'Children, teatime. Wash your hands.' She paused and looked to Pam. 'Wait for it – just watch the ratbags try to get out of it, and try *me*, and come down too soon to have plausibly washed their hands.'

At the table, Benjamin pondered through a prayer. Val served the meat. Elizabeth passed the gravy boat with the trout painted on its side. Wendy took the bowl of potatoes. Val admired Wendy's mother for having six children, though the thought made her shudder.

Val liked the children to speak mildly and entertainingly at mealtimes. Anecdotes were welcome. A few times Benjamin had brought along magic tricks. Elizabeth liked to heft that great big medical dictionary to the table and set it to one side of her plate, chewing and running a finger down page after page, wanting to be noticed. But tonight there was no dictionary, and Elizabeth sat straight in her chair.

Suddenly Val had a premonition of her daughter at a table flanked by others, a dinner in her honour, flowers in bowls.

Elizabeth and Wendy clinked their glasses of ginger ale, giggling.

Pam took up her knife and fork. 'Colleen has ideas about what we can do with the upstairs bedroom. I've got no eye for that sort of thing.'

'What about Gordon?' Val blurted out.

Pam turned. 'What about him? As a decorator?'

The sourness of the gin coated Val's mouth, making it dry. 'As a prospect. For you.'

'For me. Ah.' Pam set down her cutlery.

Val barrelled on. 'He's adventurous – god knows. Employed in a profession he likes. He's kind, good to the children.'

'Val.'

'You could both be very happy.'

'Val.'

She was breathless. 'You could live nearby, find a house together.'

Benjamin asked, 'Is he better?'

Elizabeth looked up sharply.

'Yes, how is he?' Pam added.

'Well,' Val said, 'he won't let Stuart examine him, so how are we to know?'

'But what does he *say*?'

Val stood and picked up the dish of peas from the centre of the table. She stirred them with a spoon. 'I wish I hadn't brought it up.'

She needed this night to chop away at her fears. Unwrap the lamb from the butcher's, set a pot of peas on the stove, separate the eggs for the custard. These repeated gestures would undermine the dramatics of an ill, beloved brother; the searching wonder of him alive inside a small aeroplane, threading the machine through the sky. She would remain excited, but calm. Val owed him this. So many times as children she'd upstaged him: sulking without good reason after Gordon slid first down a grassy bank. Val running away from a family picnic and getting cornered by geese. A midnight trip for the whole family to the hospital after she'd swallowed a coin.

She sat down. The girls spoke quietly to each other. Val, not at all hungry, finished her food in silence.

The square green clock above the stove said twenty minutes past eight. The house slipped into near silence in the space after tea, before the airman. Pam shook a cigarette from its packet and insisted on starting a sink full of dishes. Benjamin perched on the kitchen bench with the jug of leftover custard and a long silver spoon in his lap. He was grinning. Val let it all slide and left them there: Pam with her hands in water; her son and the spoon.

Alone, Val angled the bathroom mirror closer and drummed her fingers across her forehead. The grind of a truck lowering its gears sounded in the distance. She hoped Stuart was, right at that moment, getting into his car on Hopkins Street, pulling onto the road and heading for home.

Val pushed the mirror towards the bathroom wall, feeling as though she'd been looking skywards all day. She stuck her head into the hallway. 'It's almost time,' she called.

Elizabeth

She remembered what her uncle had told her in the woodshed: that lately he would fall asleep without any warning and wake up – it could be seconds or minutes later – feeling like his mind was a cloud. Or, had he said, *in* a cloud? When he told her, his hands weren't shaking, as he cushioned a piece of timber in his palm. He was getting better though, and she mustn't tell anyone, because her mother was a worrier at the best of times.

But he'd earnt his licence; he had shown them the papers. He'd done all those hours. Whole days at a time, and if he came over for tea afterwards, he would tell them about his lessons and what Prossers Forest looked like from the air. How nothing below seemed to move.

Elizabeth sprang up from the bedroom floor. Panic was beginning to bloom in her chest. It all threatened to fly apart. The excitement over Gordon in the aeroplane, a real aviator. Taking flight for the first time over Newstead. It could all be lost. The conditions tonight were perfect for flying – Gordon had told her so. The night was beginning to fill up. At thirteen, almost fourteen, maybe you just ended up knowing things that weren't yours to do anything about, but you had to hold on to them anyway.

From her desk she lifted the medical dictionary with two hands and tore through it, flicking pages at a time and then slowing to run her finger down. Truthfully, this part felt exciting, felt adventurous. The lolly jar now had ten shillings more. Far away, Paris was exciting, where artists painted, where spangled dancers kicked their legs across a stage. Elizabeth could draw them and find out what made their lives tick. And she would send letters home, to the white house in Launceston, letters to her mother that would say, *Look what I've done. See what I'm doing.*

'Mum?'

'I'm in the bathroom.'

Pressing the dictionary open against her chest, she left her bedroom and found her mother washing her hands at the sink. Elizabeth's feet were cold on the tiles and she shivered.

'Mum, what did you want to be when you grew up?'

'Say again, love?' Her mother turned properly and stared at the book.

'When you were my age?'

'When I was your age it was 1933.'

'Yes?'

'And things were not like that for girls.'

'Not like what?' Elizabeth felt her heart thudding beneath the pages of the book.

Her mother took a while to speak. 'Want me to make you another skirt like that one?' she asked, pointing. 'Remind me tomorrow.' She rubbed Elizabeth's shoulder and eased past.

Elizabeth watched her walk towards the stairs, the scent of her perfume persisting. Wisps of hair from her bun fell down her neck. She paused at the handrail and her shoulders went up and down.

Elizabeth's fear came upon her like an object flung from a great height. What would her mother do? Who would her mother become with another person to grieve? Her mum and uncle had lost their mother and father within a single month. Elizabeth knew her mum should know Gordon's confession about falling asleep. But she'd been told before to stay out of adult business, although not in so many words. Everything she said seemed to be wrong.

VAL

The knives and forks were lined up in rows on a tea towel, warm from the water, when Val returned to help Pam. She told Benjamin to go put on a proper jumper. He hopped down from the bench and dashed out, and Val saw that all the custard was gone.

'He's a good boy,' she said. 'Takes after his uncle.'

'Val …' Pam shook her head. 'This thing with Gordon …'

'Oh, he will be *fine.*' She slotted the knives into the drawer.

'I meant you thinking that he and I could be a pair.'

Val eased the drawer closed. She kept her eyes down. 'I know you see me as a silly housewife, with silly ideas and a boring life.'

'I do not.'

'But there's something to be said, isn't there? For fitting in and settling down and having a life that is just … simpler.'

Pam plunged her hands into the water. 'I've never put you in a position where you had to comment on my life.'

'Pammy.'

'You and I could be closer, but I've been considerate of you all these years, thinking, *No, it isn't fair to thrust that upon her.* And so we're close, yes, but I make sure Colleen is away when you visit. Have you never noticed?'

'I have, yes,' Val whispered.

'And I don't comment on your life here.'

Val looked up sharply. 'What about it?'

'Nothing, is my point. I told you a serious thing earlier about Colleen's mother and you can't even … I won't stay. I've packed for three nights, but I'll leave in the morning.'

'Pam, that's silly.' Val thought of the two slices of cake she'd set aside on a plate in the fridge. 'Look.' She tried to stop herself from crying and glanced towards the front door. 'It's almost half past eight. Quick, please. What I said. Forget it for now. Quick.'

She held out a towel. They kept their eyes down, on their two pairs of hands, touching. Val noticed the end of a cigarette smouldering in the glass ashtray. Pam reached around and lit another.

Outside, in the front yard of the house, the cool spring air chilled Val more than it should. She thought about running inside for a cardigan but didn't want to miss anything. She listened to the crickets and watched her friend standing next to the tall pine, patting her son's hair. The tip of her cigarette was a pinprick glow that danced above Benjamin's head. He leaned against Pam and his body sagged – for the first time, Val realised how late it was. She saw Pam's tenderness with her sweet, lonely boy. Who else had been there all these years except for Pam? Who else would she talk to so she didn't go mad? She'd tried to engage her husband in evening conversations to bring them closer together, but that had made her feel even lonelier. No-one's fault.

The sky beckoned.

Think about him, she willed Pam across the cold grass. Think about the life you could have with this man you have known for decades. Cure him.

ELIZABETH

In the front yard, Elizabeth walked away from Miss Loveling and Benjamin and Wendy, and went to stand at the letterbox to watch the night sky over their gabled roof. The aeroplane would come from that direction, from the north. Elizabeth thought she might snap from anticipation. She pictured the muscles in her chest. The lines of a fine drawing inside, so close to the surface. The colours of the day had gone. Across the street, the lights in the Robinsons' house were off. Dark, too, was the Tyrells' house, quiet behind its low stone fence and neatly spaced hydrangeas.

The pair of lights she saw now were confusing. So low to the ground, and from the wrong direction. She blinked and realised her father had arrived, slowing the car as it drew up to the house. More quickly than normal, her mother in her green dress dashed across the lawn and met him at the driver's window. They spoke in low tones. The click of the door opening, his unfolding out of the car. In one movement he held his hat on his head and looked upwards, beaming. Elizabeth saw her brother smile. Wendy hugged herself. Miss Loveling took off her coat and draped it across Wendy's shoulders.

More than anything, Elizabeth hoped to see the aeroplane flying overhead. The clouds and the stars would make way, and this would be the beginning of Gordon's new life, not the end.

She stood alone and waited for the sky to reveal him. The pilot and his aeroplane turning to new things in the mind's eye.

THE GARDEN BRIDGE

2009 | CAROL W. GREIDER | PHYSIOLOGY OR MEDICINE

*Prize motivation: 'for the discovery of how chromosomes
are protected by telomeres and the enzyme telomerase'*

THE SUMMER WAS LONG AND REMINDED everyone of global warming and no-one knew how to enjoy it. Lucy saw a small boy releasing water from a tap in St James's Park, his golden dog lapping at it. All across the city, galleries were full. Irritated couples and young parents with strollers prickled in agitation that others had the same idea about using the cool spaces inside the National Portrait Gallery as respite from the heat. Exhibitions were at capacity but people let out soft sighs like they were turning over in bed. No-one really paid attention to the things on the walls.

Then it was winter. Evenings arrived early and the nights were cold. London in December, one Friday afternoon. Lucy stood at the bench examining images of the lower jaw of her young patient, while the girl spat water into the yellowed sink. Her mother dashed up to Lucy, throbbing with panic.

'I don't want her to have a big, risky anaesthetic.' Mrs Paulson had wild dark hair and eyes to match.

'Well,' Lucy said, 'I'm not keen on pulling out a child's entire set of teeth without pain relief.' Four years old and with twenty teeth that needed extracting because Mrs Paulson still breastfed her through the night. Lucy forced a smile.

For the rest of the afternoon, Lucy tried to suppress her judgement. But she marvelled at the woman's carelessness. She sent the paperwork out to Genevieve, the clinic's nurse, underlining a significant discount to get the whole thing sorted. If Mrs Paulson didn't want Lucy to do it, Genevieve could suggest other clinics, some with qualified dentists, but none without risk. Lucy treated four more patients, two of whom asked, not without dignity, if they could pay another time.

She made a cup of tea. She remembered the strange message from last night that she hadn't yet answered, but pushed the thought away. She unboxed rows of extracting forceps in crackling sterile packages and slim boxes of mirrors, stowing the rubbish in the clinic's three-hundred-litre aquarium that had once kept tropical fish. She tried to scrub the sink clean.

Icy air and sharp wind – evidence of the season, no matter how short – hit Lucy and Genevieve outside the clinic at five o'clock. On Mondays, Wednesdays and Fridays, the city switched on the streetlights. Today, soft globes of light glowed along the darkening street. Lucy buttoned her coat and waved goodbye, then, remembering, turned on her heel and doubled back to see if Genevieve had rebooked the Paulson girl. Genevieve palmed her cheek, annoyed with herself; she'd do it first thing Monday.

Lucy headed for home, where she dropped her bag on the bedroom floor and went into the tiny bathroom, and took off her coat, then her cardigan, then unbuttoned her shirt, then shed her bra, and searched out the lump in her left breast with the fingers of her right hand. All day she worked on people's teeth, attended to their worries. Hour upon hour her mind tamped down on others' pain. But in the lulls between patients she met herself in the mirror of the clinic and her mind dilated with despair, remembering the corrupted cells incubating under her skin.

On Saturday afternoon, the heating having run out, Lucy finally got warm in bed, rugged up in her coat and gloves. Outside, the day was almost finished, the sky fox-burnished.

She rolled over and reached for her phone. The message. Still unanswered. It was from a man she didn't know: Jay was a fan of her father's work, he said. He loved everything her father had ever designed or helped construct. With life as grim as it was nowadays, with people lonelier than ever, he'd love to convey to Lucy how much her father's ideas meant to him. Would Lucy meet him at the Garden Bridge?

She lay staring at the ceiling, holding her phone to her chest.

She supposed Jay had found her name the regular way. Six months ago, a reporter called to ask for comment, before *The Guardian* published her father's obituary. The article labelled him a maverick, quoting those who said he was a genius, others who called him single-minded in all respects, hinting at arrogance. He never expressed publicly any regret for the Garden Bridge and what happened there.

Twenty years before that, *The New Yorker* ran a story after the money had finally been raised for a taller, grander version of the original design, financed almost entirely by a hyperactive billionaire who, Lucy's father said, couldn't tell the difference between a birch and an oak. Wind farms were an eyesore, the billionaire said more than once. But a bridge with trees would be a monument.

Construction got underway. By that stage, public opinion was no more favourable than when the idea was first floated at the start of the century. But the project would go ahead.

Lucy accompanied her father to the opening, which was on a Saturday in spring. Creamy clouds were torn in the sky. Scents from pelargoniums in their planters and swarms of snowy hawthorn stung the air. Lucy saw women in bright dresses, handsome men in pale blue shirts open at the neck. These were the celebrities who walked up and over the bridge first, holding her father's arm. Politicians disappeared among the foliage ahead. Investors frolicked behind trees.

Then, when Lucy was in high school, there was an accident. Later, she found out about the calls for better pedestrian management during peak tourist season to reduce congestion at the entrances. But these had been ignored. There was a crush and two people died – one of them a child. After the bridge reopened, others came, usually at night, to a spot in the centre of the bridge, where it was thirty metres wide and at its greatest distance from the water. Low-hanging branches worked to camouflage the intentions of people who pressed themselves against the edge like tongues, numb with pain, right before they plummeted. Of all the things that were prohibited, like sprinting and cycling and skateboarding and drinking and releasing ashes and riding a horse and flying a kite, the most dangerous activity was the one that couldn't be banned, the one the bridge became notorious for. The city erected a three-metre-high palisade fence at both ends. The rate of deaths slowed but never stopped.

Now the trees at the centre were overgrown and loveless. The flowers in their planters fought and won against neglect and continued to flourish among the weeds.

Eyes shut. A sensation of plunging, falling. Lucy opened her eyes and sat up in bed. In a row on her bedhead stood three pot plants and a photograph of her father seated at his studio desk. The leaves of a rabbit's foot fern touched her arm. Lucy thought of the garden from her childhood house, which was filled with hawthorn trees. She remembered autumns home from school, lying beside the fireplace, tipping her toes in her father's lap. He liked to balance a glass of whiskey on the arm of the sofa.

She examined the pilling on the seams of her red woollen gloves. *Okay*, she typed, *4 pm Sunday. Temple entrance.*

On Sunday afternoon at Temple Station, Lucy considered the sanity of coming alone to meet a stranger. She stepped out of the Underground. After two days at home by herself, being outside felt abrasive. She dug her gloved hands into her coat pockets. Sometimes, she found herself in public pressing her palms to her breasts. Remembering the lump was like treachery – her own mind directing her attention to something that would cause her pain to think about. Her feelings towards her body were deeply complicated. The prayer she tossed through her brain while she touched herself at the mirror wasn't *Let me live* but *Go back in time*. Pinpoint the moment the tainted cells took hold and simply *change that day*.

Commuters hurried past the pigeon-grey wall of the Tube station, heads down against the cold, bodies compact. For three or four seconds she held eye contact with a man – black hair, clean-shaven, short and powerful, eyes like liquorice – wearing a backpack and a brown jacket. And just as naturally as if they'd already met, she raised an arm and waved. It was Jay. They didn't shake hands, but he motioned for her to cross the road. They took up a spot at the handrail beside the palisade fence.

The bridge should have been beautiful, and for a time it was. Now, Lucy noticed a pair of boxy CCTV cameras peering down from the spiked top of the fence. The phone number for a suicide hotline was printed on a sign bolted at one end, and beside it, not quite blocking the space where the walkway had once been, stood an overflowing concrete bin as big as a barrel. Food wrappers, leaves and slimy twists of paper were dammed up against the base of the fence. At night, to those on the banks and to people in houseboats, the river reflected the safety lights. Some days, in the late-afternoon sun, the bridge ghosted in the windows of buildings and of buses driving by, but people's eyes skimmed right past.

'This must be a difficult place for you,' Jay said. He clasped his hands, which were shaking.

Lucy looked past him to the hanging garden. Thin coils of branches snaked to the ground.

She thought of a noose.

The truth dropped into her mind like a stone. 'You're not a fan of my father's work.' She felt short of breath, ill, as she stared at the water below. 'That isn't why you contacted me.'

'No. I'm not a fan.'

Lucy shut her eyes and felt the handrail's smooth iciness. Had she been waiting for Jay or, if not him, someone like him? Perhaps a red-raw, rain-soaked father of one of the victims – the child was Venezuelan, only eight when she died on holiday visiting her aunt and uncle. Photographs showed her cute and chubby in t-shirt and skirt, hair braided. Her family's sadness must have been immense.

A knock on her door like that – well, she expected it. She would be open to his reprimands, to the way she imagined a man from Venezuela would behave – Lucy was shameless in how narrowly she pictured this foreigner, dark and large with anger. She'd let him take her in his teeth, his grief so wide and starving.

The other victim was a pale blonde artist, all cherry lips and resin earrings, the mother of a small son. In the crush, she had suffocated.

'Who did you know?'

'My brother,' Jay said.

By that stage, her father had moved on to new projects. He hadn't spoken about the bridge for years. When the inquest report was released, Lucy read it online, hungrily. She looked up from the final page, remembering the trip to a village in Sweden when she was five or six. They crossed a bridge covered in flowers. Lucy skipped over it. Her father remained in the middle. He was the pivot point. She passed back and forth, while he made plans and visions in his mind.

A knock at the door. Let them in, the victims' families. They would glimpse the charcoal print in the hallway and her gumboots against the wall. A knock to dislodge the guilt.

'How old was he?'

'Nineteen.'

She breathed deeply. 'He could have done it on any bridge.' All her good intentions evaporating. The spectre of the Venezuelan father winking out. She felt, unaccountably, defensive. This shaking man beside her, his intimate agitation.

'Yes.'

'He could have jumped in front of a bus or shot himself,' she said. 'Or overdosed. In Ibiza. Do people still go there?'

'He could have.'

'When did it happen?' Without knowing why, she hoped it was recent.

He let out a moan, almost unnoticeable. 'Just over a year ago.'

The wind threw itself against Lucy's face. It stung her cheeks. The Thames was silver and creased in countless places. A low-slung yacht scooped along the water as Jay reached into his pocket. *A gun.* Of course. Remarkable how much she didn't mind. Only a slight fear existed inside her. Life was different now. The city was different from when Lucy was a girl. And being part of it meant letting go of old ideas about how long you got to live.

But instead, Jay brought out a cigarette. Lucy was surprised to feel relieved. He offered her one, which she declined. He cupped his hands, sparked the flint and waited for the flame to catch. The cigarette lighter was old-fashioned, red plastic with a half-chipped-off logo. Coca-Cola? Most of these lighters had been banned, along with plastic toothbrushes and thousands of other objects, which transformed into depressingly sturdy vessels that pitched on waves and sieved down the gullets of humpbacks.

The list of things she missed was incredibly long; plastic toothbrushes were almost nothing. She'd been a child at boarding school before the worst of it happened. Memories of the extravagance, but also the simplicity: bowls of cream, pyramids of scones, platters of thick pink fish, three different types of rice. Papaya and oranges so plentiful the girls arranged slices into patterns on plates to pass the time at dinner before sweeping the fruit into the bin. She remembered it all with shame and hunger.

Jay smoked, bowing his head towards the water. These days, he told her, he smoked *and* meditated. The trick with meditating was to understand the brain could be treated like a muscle that responded to training and repetition.

'Returning to the void is the challenge. Meditation will save me,' he joked. Jay exercised as much as possible and tried to limit his worries. He would live for decades, perhaps. It was a cheery thing to say, but Jay didn't seem cheerful. When he turned his face up to her, he grinned, showing perfect white teeth. She thought of the Paulson girl, the rot she had inherited.

'Nobody needed it,' Jay said. 'This should never have been built.'

He told her that boys from their neighbourhood assumed he and his brother, Dima, were rich. Dima's Russian name, their father's slick black hair. Dima liked all that mystery.

'He pretended a lot. His whole life. He could have been anything,' Jay said. 'When we were kids, he loved breaking something apart, looking inside, rebuilding it from scratch, showing the others. But a different product at the end. A computer changed. A battery made smaller.'

Jay stubbed out the cigarette, swung his backpack around and unzipped its mouth. Opened the bag. A dark cavity.

'What—' she started.

But then Lucy saw: something homemade, something deadly, something that would have impressed those neighbourhood boys.

'Whatever happens,' he said, 'they won't rebuild it.'

She imagined the phone calls this time – from newspapers and radio stations, catching her live on-air. She was terrified of it all. Nothing felt safe.

'I wanted to give you one last chance to see it,' he said, not touching the explosives.

She would go to Sweden.

In the kitchen of her flat, Lucy filled a can and watered the row of African violets on the windowsill. Perhaps if she didn't return, a person walking on the street below would notice them flourishing.

She left, taking very little. She paused outside, keys in hand, when a moment of nostalgia ballooned inside her. But she hadn't lived there for long – less than a year – and the nostalgia subsided. She shouldered her duffel bag. She locked the door.

Yes, toffee-coloured Stockholm would do. Lucy yearned for a place away from London's unlit lanes and whiffy air, the grimy pavements and sour people who were tetchy with panic and oftentimes hunger. Some days she could barely see the lid of the sky. Too much pain at the clinic, too much drudgery and uncertainty to ruminate on each night. The promise of this new destination was now a bridge of a different sort, a tremendous light-filled opportunity. Less her father's failed garden path connecting two halves of a divided city than an elegant suspension bridge spanning a before and an after – a slender piece of steel. She didn't know if it would hold, if such a thing were possible. But the challenge would have tempted her father.

Now, possibilities trod through her like footfalls. She reached out to this future, however long it would last, in whatever form her body took.

At St Pancras, Lucy paused at a screen showing CCTV pictures. She'd last glimpsed Jay by the tall fence, a shadow gaining a foothold. Investigators were searching for this man – here, his frozen black-and-white image – as well as a woman with long brown hair, seen talking with him before the attack. The chaos of aerial footage of police cars hastily parked. Lucy saw a bite taken out of the belly of the corrupted bridge. A dark space existed now where Jay's bomb must have exploded, looking like a door through which a man might disappear, and then his brother, and then a woman after them.

THE TOWN TURNS OVER

2014 | MAY-BRITT MOSER | PHYSIOLOGY OR MEDICINE

Prize motivation: 'for their discoveries of cells that constitute a positioning system in the brain'

I F YOU WANT TO KNOW how we got here, we will tell you. Once, not so long ago, we were everybody's ageing parents. We lived in nursing homes, aged care facilities, places called Freedom Villas. These were not always good places. Politicians loved coming to visit for morning tea, bringing their own cups. Thankfully our children visited too. They are good people – we've raised them well. Most of them are parents now. Somehow this has happened.

— My word, Marilyn says, it's strange seeing your own children parent: the same thing giving them the shits that once gave you the shits.

— But also, Oliver says, the very creatures who brought love into your life get to see how magical it is.

We nod. Oliver is a real softie.

Most of our grandchildren are lovely. Most, by this stage of our lives, are teenagers. All of them: busy bees, lots on their plates. They came to visit as often as they could. The girls turned up wearing sneakers and tiny denim shorts and shirts that were basically bras.

— But we loved it! We weren't prudish about it!

— Absolutely not!

—We were prudish about nothing!

None of us is leery (well, except for Marshall, but he can't move quickly). No, to those beautiful teenage girls we wanted to say (and some of us did), *Oh, to be your age. You look gorgeous. Your skin — see how it returns to its shape after you press it like this? You're glowing! Enjoy that, please.*

The boys, the best ones, our beautiful grandsons, we watched them carefully to see if they carried their mothers' grocery bags into our Freedom Villas. We smiled when they searched for the best place to put our shaving cream, our barley sugars, our incontinence pads. We saw the muscles of their arms flex and their calves contract as they crouched to the ground. They didn't quite know where to put their hands or how to embrace us.

—Anywhere is fine! Eleanor says.

—That's right, Marilyn says. *Come here*, we would say. *Give your nan a hug.*

In their bodies, we remembered our own games of cricket and netball, the snap of a bathing cap at the pool and the pummel of water when we dived in. We remembered walking long distances with no destination in mind, or speeding up to catch the bus to work. Our bodies, the machinery, it was all understood and it all *worked.*

— Mabel here wants to say something.

— All right, Oliver says, let her speak.

— I feel such a lightness here, Mabel says, in this place. And in my head. This isn't a bad thing. There's an *awakeness*, isn't there?

—You must take time to sleep each day, Mabel. You have to try.

Across the expanse of our beach, we've set up a dozen spots where we can sleep. Vito takes Mabel by the arm and steers her towards a nest made ready. Sleep comes at different times for us all.

Since we began to wander some of us developed a theory that rather than making us sleepier, the wandering – the getting lost – released something in our brains.

— Like a mechanism.

— It's *all* mechanisms, Sarah says, gesturing her soft and wrinkled hands up and down her body.

What we're trying to say is that we've never felt so awake.

Let one of us explain. Eleanor is good at it.

— She's very clear, yes.

— Precise, and not at all condescending.

— It would be my pleasure, Eleanor says. What happened was this: lots of people were living in our town.

— Lots of *old* people.

— That's right, Eleanor continues. And I'll happily use that word: *old*. I see no problem with it. It's a beautiful spot, that town. The turtles go there in the summer, lay their eggs. You can go down in the middle of the night with torches if you're quiet enough. A lot of us get rather caught up with those turtles and their eggs when they begin to hatch, with the plight of hundreds of tiny animals about to face the sea. The town where we come from is close to here, to this island. It has nice parks, plenty of cafes, a cinema—

— Cheap Tuesdays!

—Yes, all that. Well, one day, about two months ago, something began to happen, across all our brains.

— It might have been the tides, Vito says.

—Tides have been here longer than any of us, Brian says.

— It was a daytime event at first, Marshall chimes in. Something we did in the daytime.

— No-one knows for sure the exact *reason*, Eleanor says. But

Sarah used to be head of nursing at Townsville Public. And she's tried her best to piece things together and do her own research. You know how computers work? Well, it's something like our very own inner positioning—

— GPS-related, Marilyn says.

— Yes, just like that. It changed. Our brains changed.

— And we began to wander.

Putting aside the tides or the moon, here's what we think: events of a lifetime accrue in our brains like calcium. Like radium, settling in our bones, a never-ending half-life. The brain can only take so much. Sometimes, in our Freedom Villas, we were left for hours, bladder-pinched, our bones aching in the dark. Thirsty at noon with a jug of water just out of reach, and a call button that may as well have been connected to our very own breastbones – but enough of that.

Even the good stuff weighs you down before it hollows you out. Our entire planet – every thought that's ever been had, every deed – is determined, controlled and organised by the brain, by what we cannot see. Trillions upon trillions of messages back and forth, if old age is where you find yourself. Well, our brains began to misfire and all the old faces, and the doorways and hallways in our homes, and streets and patterns in the outside world, they became a puzzle. And, for us, it was a puzzle we had no great desire to complete. Like: why were we so intent on *solving* it when we could just wander and be with one another? Find clarity. We got lost when we couldn't find our way to the end.

We hear there's going to be a meeting in town. Some of us crowd around one another, burying our feet in the sand, and we're able to see the meeting.

— Okay, Eleanor starts. Let me—

— Yes, Lupita says, this part is hard to explain.

— The vision, Don says. The town turning over while we are not there.

— Somehow it is visible to us, Lupita says. The brain is a wonderful thing. That's what they told us at our Freedom Villas. And now we believe it.

— It's marvellous fun!

— Even though sometimes it fizzles in and out, like a wireless. So, you see, we cannot explain it. But we can *see* it.

Frida, who runs the bar at the RSL on weekends, is taking around platters of eggplant dip and haloumi skewers. Ursula from the newsagent is there, Toni from the fish and chip shop, Cameron and his four rib-eye sons who have a monopoly on all domestic and civic garden maintenance. A few of the local teachers are there. Rick the electrician, who always takes up two parking spaces at Freedom Villas instead of one.

— But he's always fair. As honest as the day is long, Brian says.

We watch the part of the meeting when Bob stands, clears his throat and says, 'It's all very strange, yes. But ... Marilyn, my mother-in-law, has been missing for almost a week ... what I'm saying is: maybe we should let sleeping dogs lie.'

'Bob!' His wife, Cindy, is a tall and powerful woman who strikes him on the thick of his back, right above the rump. Bob sits down. We look over at Marilyn. She is lying on her belly beneath a casuarina, reading an old copy of *Frankenstein* that somebody else – maybe Ken – brought along. We feel bad for her. She frowns at something in the book, licks her thumb and turns the page.

— King of the mother-in-law jokes, Marilyn says, without looking up. What a genius he is.

— Cindy got stuck with him, Sarah says, didn't she? But she could have gotten out. There was still time. Nothing is set in stone, even after you have children.

We return to the vision. Marilyn flips a page of her book.

'It all boils down to this,' Frida says. 'How do we keep our goddamn parents alive?'

'We must make this town safe,' Niamh the kindergarten teacher says. 'They could wander down to the ocean like *that*.' She clicks her fingers.

Cameron shakes his head. 'They must be absolutely terrified.'

'Cameron, some of them fought in Korea,' Janey the high-school teacher says drily. We know that she refused to pay Cameron to do her yard. 'I reckon they'll be all right.'

— Oh, bless that sensible Janey, Eleanor says.

We all know the story of a colleague of Janey's who drove his mother to a cottage in the Tablelands and locked the door so she couldn't escape. The son turned up at the house the next morning to find she'd hitched back to town.

— Never mind that he could have stayed with her all night, Lupita says. Spent *time* with her?

— I have something to add, Denise says.

She is weaving palm fronds, making a bowl.

— Yes, go on, Denise. Please do.

— When Andrew was nine months old, I couldn't leave him, not for a minute, could not walk out that door because if I did he held his breath till he passed out. Talk about inner positioning. That baby knew where I was every second of the day. It was like he watched me through the nursery walls, lying there behind the bars of his cot, just plotting my movements around the house.

— Oh, Denise, you poor thing.

At the meeting, we watch Andrew slide a cube of haloumi from the skewer into his mouth. We feel sorry for Denise, who for many years was caught up in disputes with neighbours about recalcitrant dogs, and fences, and garbage bins, and parking along the yellow line outside her driveway, right up until she got lost, to be with us here. Oliver squeezes Denise's elbow. She drops the palm frond bowl, reaches for a green plastic bucket and lays the foundation of a sandcastle between her feet. Beside her, Ken and Lupita hold tree branches in their laps. They sharpen the ends with their small red knives.

— So, my son can just give me a minute now, Denise says. He can give me a mile. No-one's passing out. I'm sure as hell not. It's a very sinister sort of captivity to be in your nice home that you've designed and kitted out with appliances and soft cushions. You're trapped. You'd claw your way out of there if you could. And I couldn't, not for about three years. And all of this would be fine if there was an end to the worry parents feel. But there isn't. It doesn't let up. Not for your whole life.

— Oh, *Andrew*, we all say, though he cannot hear us.

Ken and Lupita put down their knives, and pat Denise on the leg, one each.

Marshall has done some eggs for our tea, Mabel has done the chops. We hear rumblings that they're coming for us. That the end is nigh. But that could be a false feeling our brains are feeding us. Ken hands around the plates and offers to slice the meat for those who need it. Mabel garnishes the chops with tufts of pigface and we spread across the sand, easing down to sit and eat.

Look, we all had disparate experiences in our earlier lives. We mentioned Denise's difficulties with her neighbours. Sarah lost a son to a terrible fight with a stranger on a foreign beach. Don founded a company that he later sold for $120 million. Lupita adopted dogs that nobody else wanted, and one even saved her life. We've had first children and second children and lost children and final babies that turned out to be our last (many of us have agreed this was like settling into a body of water that initially shocked us, frightened us, but turned out to give us great pleasure and joy). The things going on in our brains that make us wander are difficult to explain, but *look*! Look how happy we are, now that we don't know where we are going.

The next day starts off normal enough, but by dusk we can all feel it. Something's not quite right. Vito loses his footing on a tree root. Marilyn eats a mandarin and pith gets caught in her throat, almost choking her. Denise wakes from her afternoon nap to realise she has lost her voice. Looking at one another, we think but do not say: *Is this the end? Is someone coming for us?*

We are lying in the sand. The sun is sending up great big swathes of colour into the sky. A sharp breeze sluices through the air. When those of us who like to observe boats and ships see them out on the water, we wave the others over. Watching a ship, even with the naked eye, is telescopic. It acts to minuscule us even further. Who is at the controls of that ship right now? What do they see when they gaze back across the seal-grey ocean that laps upon our beach? Do they imagine we are a 'lost tribe' that might show up on the evening news?

Lupita and Brian are propped up on their sides, facing each other. They have their feet in the water. Oliver wears a wreath of pigface and gum leaves twisted around his head. Marilyn sits back on her heels with a pile of sand heaped in front of her. Sarah joins her and they drag their hands through the wet sand. They build a moat. We agree how lovely the grit of sand is in the webbing of our fingers.

— Someone told me once, Eleanor says, that there are more atoms in a grain of sand than there are stars in the universe.

— Oooh, Ken says, I think you've got that a bit wobbly.

— But who's going to know? Marshall asks.

— There's no way to prove any of that, Denise says.

— Lovely thought, though, Vito adds.

We agree it's a lovely thought. Ideas like this keep us watered and fed.

We hear a shout, then twigs snapping.

The woman is young. Gorgeous round hips. Lovely smile, curly dark hair. The man is short. Small flat nose. His eyes are generous and sooty-dark. He wears a footy jersey and black socks and sneakers; she is in jeans turned up at the ankles and a rain mac. The two of them come round the edge of the beach where the island's sand dips away towards the forest. We watch them. They are both wet to the knees. Our breathing syncs up: that part we know.

'We found you,' the man says.

They have found us.

'Whoa, there are a lot of you, aren't there!'

'You're safe now,' the woman says, slowly. 'I'm Paula. This is Jason.'

'We'll show you the way home,' Jason says. 'You must be freezing.'

'Here.' Paula holds out a hand.

Mabel rolls onto her back. She resembles a pale, uncooked pastry dusted in sugar. She looks up at the sky. She raises her arms above her head and makes a snow angel in the sand.

'Let's get you home,' Jason says.

— No, thank you, Mabel tells him, then to the woman: I know you. I used to clean your mother's house.

'Mrs Jeffrey,' Paula says, reaching for her. 'If they find you, it won't be pretty. Please let us help you.'

— Okay, Mabel says, making great sweeping swirls with her arms.

We watch Jason and Paula watching her. 'Please,' Paula urges. 'Better to come with us. Jason and I are the good guys.'

'We can sort everything out once we're off the island, hey? Once we're back?' Jason says.

— There's nothing to sort, Vito says. We've made our goodbyes.

— Thanks, love, but this is it for us, Eleanor says.

Jason doesn't seem to have heard. 'But another day or so and the Freedom Villas people will find you.'

— They won't find us.

Vito is forceful.

— That is a promise, my dear, Lupita tells her.

Paula opens and closes her mouth. She takes a step back. Jason scratches his head. Sarah has removed her coat and slippers. Her blouse with the delicate blue stripes, made sheer by the water, sticks to her chest. The young ones don't know where to look. But we are entirely comfortable. This is yet another experience that will become a layer in our brains.

Out to sea a container ship eases through the water, along the line of the horizon. It looks like a toy being pulled by a child.

The waves rock and suck around Ken's ankles. Lupita moves to his side and they crouch in the shallows, their temples together. We watch them whispering. Lupita leans down and dips her knife into the water, swirls it round.

LITTLE FLY

2015 | TU YOUYOU | PHYSIOLOGY OR MEDICINE

*Prize motivation: 'for her discoveries concerning
a novel therapy against Malaria'*

SEE HER THERE, THE BABY girl on the sand. Above her, her brother sits on a rock with his toes pointed towards the sea. Their parents are nearby. Watch as the woman, her mother, lifts the baby to her face and breathes and kisses, and smiles happiness, and the infant reflects it back, this joy, this love. The man, her father, scoops his hands around her on the sand. He picks up a shell and brings it to his nose then rolls it in his palm.

The baby has a secret.

Just yesterday the baby learnt her name, but today she cannot remember it. She hopes someone (her mother is her favourite) will say it again. She will listen closely and single it out among all the other sounds her mother makes, and try to hold on to it the way her father holds that shell. Her hands are behaving marvellously today – very wriggly and clenchy – and she can almost get them to do what she wants.

Her mother is a beautiful apparition, glinting in and out of her vision. She glows. They watch each other for as much time as the boy, her always-moving brother, will allow. Sometimes the mother appears very suddenly in the baby's face with a *Dooooh!*

or an *Eyaaaah!* and that's fun, especially if she lifts her up and they squish cheeks together. When that happens, the baby never wants her feet to return to the earth. At night, the baby sleeps alone, a little sad to be away from her mother and father, instead tucked up in her own bed tightly. There she dreams of strips of colour that peel away and stream downwards, meaning everything. Like the small breakaway flap on the wallpaper in their kitchen where her parents park her in a bouncer. The baby loves to spend time watching the flap, hoping to rip at it one day, hoping no-one else gets to it first. But neither the bouncer nor the torn paper exists here in this new place. They are on holiday. She hopes the paper is not gone forever.

~

This morning the family sits on one of the resort's lawns beneath palm trees and eats breakfast from a basket. Across the lawn another boy appears, this one with beautiful brown eyes and black hair neat on his scalp like a cap. He comes to them and bows at the baby's mother and father, then lays beaded necklaces around each of their necks. Her brother has his fingers on his father's beads. He wants to follow this unknown child back into the resort. The mother supposes his family works here. The brother unwraps himself from his father's hand. His father tries to explain that the other boy is working, but that sounds silly. The brother slips off the picnic rug and moves towards the kitchen. He is five, and he wants to play. All the days on holiday where he has played with just his mother and father and his baby sister, which so far had seemed fine, now feel so tedious. A kid his own age is what he needs.

~

Sometimes the baby's mother opens her mouth and words come out, and the baby replies, giving her opinion, or changing the subject if she wants to point out something that's been overlooked. Once, the mother wore a ribbon in her hair, tied high in a bow. They must have spoken about it for at least two minutes, the baby sharing her affection and delight at its floppiness and the way it shimmered in the light. Sometimes the baby's father's lips part and words come out quickly, but to a tune, which is called a song. The baby has come to recognise her favourites: the ones about lambs, about cake, about apples. She follows these along – coming as they can out of nowhere, her father busy doing something else entirely when he decides a song is what they need. They are all quite lovely – the baby swims and gurgles in their currents.

Often at home, when she knows her brother is playing and lurking about, the baby will stay quiet a little longer in her cot, pretending to be asleep. Make no mistake: she loves him. But the baby must preserve her energy, and her brother likes to jump out from the doorway to yell *Bah!* when she's lying on her back on the floor of the kitchen, having a good kick on the rug. A very vulnerable position. Her bedroom is safer: dim with four walls the colour of the sky. The small square window above the rocking chair looks out over a lake in the house that is their real home. In the chair where she drinks milk, she clasps her mother's breast or her mother's finger. This is for her mother's sake, to anchor her to the chair. A grip that says *Stay*, something the baby can convey with her fingers, and her mother seems to understand.

~

In the morning, after breakfast, the two boys see each other. One has a Coke and offers the other a sip. They kick a ball between them on the gravel behind the boat shed.

'My name is Oskar,' her brother says. 'I'm five.'

'Arif,' the other boy says. 'I'm eight.'

~

At noon the baby and her mother sit by the swimming pool on a sun lounger. Neither is quite ready for a nap yet, although the baby is full and happy, satisfied and sleepy. Above them, the sun disappears behind grey clouds. There is something brewing that the baby does not yet know, a grand and wonderful discovery that will emerge out of chaos.

Quickly. A story.

One that her mother is reading right now in a magazine, while a waiter brings her a glass of beer the colour of honey. A story about another baby, and about the writer Mary Shelley. When Shelley was sixteen she kept a diary. She became pregnant. For three days after she gave birth, she wrote about her baby's sleeping patterns and how often it fed. What it smelt like (the baby herself notices how hungrily *her* parents like to smell the top of her head). Then less than two weeks later Shelley wrote: *Find my baby dead.*

At this line, the mother marks her place in the magazine and lays it down. She rubs the toes of her daughter, who is propped between her legs on the sun lounger, examining the ears of a cloth bunny with her gums. Her mother runs a hand across her warm and fuzzy head. The sun reappears. A tall brown body dives into the water with a splash.

The baby girl does not know this Mary Shelley story yet, of course, but it will be one that she returns to time and again when she is older, having found a book in the library of the first university she attends – a reproduction of Shelley's diary where she logged her ideas, keeping her thoughts under control while she created chaos on the page. The simplicity of that final line will hit her hard: *I awoke in the night to give it suck it appeared to be sleeping so quietly that I would not awake it.* The next morning she wrote: *Find my baby dead.* The thundering horror, surely. *So quietly.*

And years later – many years even after the baby has rubbed her own mother's toes beneath a hospice blanket and years after her father's final bony embrace sends her wheeling with thickening panic out to her car to cry – when they read her name, when she collects her medal from the stage of the Stockholm Concert Hall, when the brother who loves her is in the audience, she will recall Mary Shelley's grief. She will recall the statistics and numbers set against the life she has lived and the research work she herself set out to do. One in four million. One in six thousand. One in eight hundred. One in twelve.

~

In the kitchen of the resort, Arif busies past the chefs and his mother, who stirs *soto ayam* on the stove. It is noisy and steamy. His chest feels light when his mother calls out, '*Saya sayang kamu, Arif!*' The fluorescents above the shiny steel benches seem to strobe in his vision.

Then.

On a near-empty, scrubbed-down bench, a female mosquito alights from the long slender handle of a pitcher of water, and begins to swerve through the steam. The mosquito is quick to anger and very loud. She is observant, here in the kitchen. She moves as though she is looking for holes in the fabric of the air. She flies towards the tables of the restaurant.

~

It is dinnertime. The hotel restaurant is housed beneath large beams of wood that peak in the centre of the room. Colourful flags hang from the walls. There are shells in frames, and stretched batik paintings. Tables and chairs surround three buffet stations with heat lamps and piles of ice bedding platters of prawn sambal, rice, and salads served on banana leaves. A long line of doors is open onto a verandah that is lush with a view of swaying trees, the pool and beach beyond. The baby's family sits on the verandah. At six o'clock, the restaurant is mostly empty except for families with children wired from hunger and the day's heat. The baby watches her sunburnt brother bouncing in his chair. Her father pats the boy's head, which bumps up and down beneath his hand. It's a funny thing that the baby notices, then her mother becomes aware of it too. The boy exaggerates it now. To make his mother laugh. Hearing this, the baby cackles too.

She sees the boy from the restaurant carrying plates to one end of the buffet. A white cloth hangs over his shoulder.

'That's Arif,' her brother says and waves.

The baby sees a black spot tilting in her vision. It hovers. An insect.

The baby knows she was once as big as a bug. Imagine that: all of her – flesh, bone, nail, desire – no bigger than this mosquito. She recalls when she was the size of her pinky toe, then as big as her fist, her whole being nothing larger than her chambered heart. All of her was there, growing steadily, pushing out against the plush darkness of her mother's insides. The cells of her brain multiplying, noticing light beams and blood, hearing two heartbeats, fluid rushing all around.

~

The mosquito zips so skittingly it's as though the air is something to avoid. The smooth continuation of her life depends on her capacity to find, to plunge, to withdraw blood. In this room's contours of light, she notices her hunger. First she must find a membrane. She torques with single-mindedness towards the flesh of the baby. Touches the air with her nervy wings.

~

Arif sees the mosquito or, rather, he sees movement occurring like a tiny rip in his vision, a line drawn in the air. He holds his vision on the mosquito zipping towards the baby. He reaches for it and bats it away with the back of his hand.

~

The baby swats away a feeling that her world has been changed. The connection she feels with the world around her – peace and wetness, warmth and cold, her mother tugging at the webbing of her toes to pull out bits of wool stuck there from her blanket, her father running his fingers across her scalp – is rocked. The baby feels her life starting again, in the way it does after each sleep, after each deep drink of milk. But there's been no nap or milk. There's just the boy from the restaurant, wearing a rope of beads that she longs to clench at, darting past her shoulder. He has sent something small out of her life and she is reset.

Her whole existence just coming into focus now. Seams stitching together, adults towering over her and offering her mushy fruit, faces skin to skin, knowing her and warming her with their pleasing faces and their bodies, which she recognises as matched to her own, a prayer of certainty that she is someone to be loved and understood. While from the other side of the table her mother catches her eye and gives her such a smile that the baby forgets about the danger and no longer fears what it might have done to her, or all the other numberless hazards of the world – not infection nor wildfires nor tall flights of stairs nor cancer nor a terrorist's bomb nor any sharp unfulfilment of her own line of genes – because her mother opens her mouth and says a word and *yes*, now, there it is. Yes, she catches her name and she holds it tight.

THE FIX

2018 | DONNA STRICKLAND | PHYSICS

Prize motivation: 'for their method of generating high-intensity, ultra-short optical pulses'

S HE SHOULD HAVE SAID NO when they rang to say there'd been a cancellation. No clean clothes for the kids, Neil away for three days, barely any sick leave accrued. And something beneath that – fear? Just small, like a new muscle not fully formed. In the end, *Sure* is what she tells the receptionist on the phone.

'And there's even a discount,' the receptionist adds, in an accent Tess can't pinpoint. Then the woman falters. Has she already said that? About the discount? Sorry. Hectic day!

Tess learns that because the other patient had paid half but decided at the last minute not to go through with the procedure, the doctor will pass on this discount to Tess. At this show of generosity, she traces the lower lid of her left eye. She lays down the phone and, in fact, covering both her eyes, begins to weep. She rings her sister, Cate, who sounds jubilant. She'll be on the next train up from Sydney, bringing something for the kids' dinner.

In theatre prep, they have Tess take off her wedding ring and earrings. She clips shut the glasses case Samuel made for her in Scouts. Maybe she'll turn it into a mobile phone case. She puts it away with the rest of her things in her handbag, which she slides into the locker the nurse directs her to. A ripple shakes through Tess's body. Is this the precipice? Is it really this simple? The end of something, and the beginning of something else, a future of perfect vision?

The nurse – barely older than a teenager – studies her. The young woman's lips are tight together and she smiles.

Tess allows herself a giddy moment, here with this pretty nurse she'll never see again. Tess bends towards her with the warmth of conspiracy and asks, 'Is this really happening? I was told six months minimum.'

'Must be your lucky day,' the nurse says. 'Buy yourself a lotto ticket.'

Afterwards the nurse dresses her eyes in two clear plastic patches criss-crossed with tape. 'Here.' She presses a pair of thick black sunglasses into Tess's hands. 'You'll need these. Wear them outside, whenever you need the comfort.'

'I feel fantastic!' Tess tells her.

The nurse is filling out a form on the computer and giving her instructions about rest, about swelling, about warning signs. But Tess isn't paying attention, is watching the screen, agog at how much she can see. The nurse drones on about some people experiencing dry eyes or pain, and is offering her a follow-up appointment on Monday, and telling her that if she experiences *xyz* she must call her GP. The nurse says she might be lucky and recovery might be quick, but *this*, Tess thinks. This is at the speed of light. Tess explains that her sister is at home, waiting to take care of her, that she'll get a lift home, no sweat.

They let her walk right on out of there.

She orders an Uber and the driver – young, sharp nose, slim

moustache – points at her eyes. She gives two big thumbs up. She asks him to drop her off in town at the express IGA. Inside, mingling with the after-work crowd, she heaves a bouquet of gerberas out of a bucket of water – bright droplets catch the halogens above the magazine rack – to give to her sister. Wow, the light in here. She runs her sneaker across the polished wooden floor. Getting carried away, she even feels the aeons and aeons that went into *this* piece of timber, and that one over there, in all their rich bronze glory. Into the shopping basket she tosses packets of lollies for the kids and a bag of cotton balls just in case her eyes take a turn for the worse. Somehow, because recovery is going so well so far, something in her wants to overcompensate, be ultra prepared and have to never, ever open that bag of cotton balls. Let it sit in the cupboard beneath the bathroom sink like a fat symbol of smugness. Tess smooths a tendril of tape that is coming loose from her right eye patch. She taps her credit card, blinking and grinning at the boy behind the register, who blinks right back.

When she orders another ride, it connects her straight away, and a moment later she spots him, the same Uber guy, still in the drop-off zone, scrolling through his phone that is hooked up to the dash.

She knocks on the passenger window. 'Another miracle today!'

He looks up at her, and she notices the fluorescence of the colours on the dashboard. The odometer is ablaze. The numbers of the digital radio station are *speaking* to her. The brightness of the colours registers as *volume*. Pow! He's staring, obviously not knowing about all the miracles. She buckles herself in. She will explain. A good guy. She should set him up with her sister.

Tess drops the bag of groceries at her feet. She points to the cotton balls and then to her face. 'I promise I won't bleed in here!'

The driver goes, 'Uh,' and turns away from her to pinch at an app on his phone.

All right, Tess thinks. Too much.

At home, she sees that Cate has tidied the house, hung out the laundry and made dinner. A whole ham. It glows pink and orange-golden with cloves darted through the scored skin.

'Like Christmas,' Cate says. She wears a zipped-up pale pink exercise jersey, tight black leggings with sheer panels down the side. Her tummy is flat. She's always had great legs.

Tess concentrates on the ham. She has never seen a ham this vibrant. 'That thing is glowing. Imagine not being able to see *ham* in this way. Can *you* see the ham in the way I'm seeing it?'

'I guess so,' Cate says.

The kids pile into Tess's lap. She notices they've strung up white balloons around the cornices of the dining room. They've drawn enormous blue and black eyes onto the balloons with felt pens. Eyelashes run away from the irises like spiders' legs.

'We weren't sure,' Cate says, playing with a loose string hanging from the ceiling. 'Is it too much? Too body horror?'

'Oh, no. I love them,' Tess says, prodding one with her index finger. 'They're perfect. No other balloons would do.'

There's a gap of silence till Samuel suddenly yells out, 'Surprise!' and they all laugh.

They sit around the table, Samuel at Tess's right side but practically in her lap again, then Cressy who is wearing the same dress from yesterday, then Joseph who rubs pumpkin through his hair, then Cate. The pumpkin is doing something to her senses, doing something where Tess can taste it and see it but also, like, *empathise* with it?

'That's a bright orange colour!' she tells Cate, her eyes stuck on the vegetable. Joey stares at her then flings his head back and yells – she assumes – with ecstasy.

After dinner, Neil rings from the conference. Samuel and Cressy race to speak to him, their attentive father. Tess can tell by the way they slow and listen, nodding and not saying much, that he has crafted something special and individual to say to them all.

Finally she gets the phone back and takes it into the hallway, past the kids' baby photos, and her and Neil's wedding ones.

'Love, how'd you go?' His voice is eager and kind. 'You all right?'

She notices that her wedding gown in the picture no longer looks old and tired, but proper snowy white against the bark of a tree where they'd done the photos in Centennial Parklands. Autumn. She finds her voice again in front of the mirror. She blinks at her reflection. 'Neil, I feel amazing.'

Tess wakes in the early hours summoned not by the baby, who hasn't made a sound, but by a desperate need for painkillers. She pads down the hall in her socks, incanting, *This is fine, this is normal*, knowing only too well how quickly she has latched on to the idea that she's a wunderkind, already slated to appear on some talk show where that handsome TV doctor will pop out and give her the gold medal for Best Laser Eye Surgery Patient. She takes two Panadol, then sits in the moonlit front sunroom, covering and uncovering her eyes, trying to trick her brain into disgorging any secrets that it has, up until this point, withheld.

Her vision is still gleaming. Just painful. That's all.

No sounds from the children in their rooms, or from Cate, who is asleep on Cressy's floor. Back in her own bed she spreads out and cuddles the doona. She touches Neil's soft, cool side and his pillow.

They've been married for eighteen years. *Eighteen years*, Tess thinks, always frailed a little by the vastness of it.

Outside, the wind makes a sound like crashing waves. Flurries slither through a gap in the window. She steadies her breathing and slips into sleep and a kind of hallucination where Samuel is once again an upturned-nose, glinty-eyed newborn. He and Tess are once again that single creature that lumped about Katoomba wrapped up in a puffy coat. They are setting out for the walking trail towards the Three Sisters. Tess is terribly afraid of rounding a corner badly and slipping in mud, of losing her footing and taking her son with her. She fears the mountain's edge and the cascade of spiny branches below. She kicks out to stop herself falling.

And wakes.

Rubbing a hand across her face, moving her fingers gently around the eye patches, she sees a new vision. A black SUV drives up towards the mountains, along the Great Western Highway, at the end of a winter's day when the sun is loud and blazing. Bunches of stone-grey leaves in the tall gums shake and twinkle like cheerleaders' pom-poms. The car is Neil's – Samuel's clicky-clacky macrame fish from Scouts dangles from the rear-view mirror. A feeling grips Tess around the chest, an exquisite rubbery tightening. She is seized, vice-like. Her breathing shallows, and she sees the car plunging on in the dark. There are points of light and the sound of brakes. A perfect deer that has been alone on the road is alone no longer. In its rusted brown coat, it dashes off and almost gets away. But not quite. Tess sees the pearly, wet swell of bone on black.

Then an icy whoosh beside her – doona billowing, sheets parting – and a body is in the bed.

'I drove,' Neil says. 'I should have been here for you.'

The bone on the bitumen. Tess reaches to touch his hands. 'Are you okay?' she asks.

But before he says another word, he moves in behind her back, his cold hands gripping her soft belly, his erection at her back. She has her pyjama pants off, expertly, in seconds then wedges her underpants down the mattress with the sole of her foot. He reaches in between her legs, and they both shudder at her readiness.

He's finished in minutes and, for once, so is she. She lies back. She knuckles at her breastbone. She is happy for him to hear her sped-up breath while she reaches backwards in time to try to remember the last time the sex was this good, this focused, this fastened on one another's pleasure, and her on her own.

Finally, Neil swallows thickly in the dark. Tess wonders what he will say.

'Show me your eyes, love. Turn on the light.'

In the morning, before the baby or anyone else wakes, Tess knots her thick pink dressing-gown around her waist and moves in her slippers down the hallway towards Cressy and Cate's room. A fear flickers: the volume of her and Neil's lovemaking? Her sister in the house? But Tess is relieved when she sees the door has been stuck firmly shut, presumably all night.

She makes herself a cup of tea in the silent kitchen. She catches sight of herself in the door of the fat-spackled microwave. Her hair is flat and lanky. Her eye patches are shiny, bug-like, and behind them the pain is coming on, tidal. She buffs an oval section of the kitchen window sheer with her palm and gazes out at the frosted lawn. Samuel's red football shorts yell from the clothesline. Neil's black SUV is dewdrop-beaded. She leans closer until her eye patches kiss the glass. Something – is it wet? pulpy? – is stuck to the bumper of her husband's car. She takes her mug and sets out across the gravel to get a closer look.

A BRIEF HISTORY OF PETROLEUM

2018 | FRANCES H. ARNOLD | CHEMISTRY

Prize motivation: 'for the directed evolution of enzymes'

IT BEGAN WITH NAOMI IN chemistry class, helping me with my homework. I wasn't failing but I wasn't diligent either, at that time preferring to do nothing over something. Our grade twelve teacher was American, and she and I clashed about all sorts of stuff, but in a way that made me think we were intellectual equals. Mrs Cline would say to the class, *Gee, it's hot out.* She'd say, *Energy can only be transferred or transformed.* She'd say, *Think about the environmental impact.*

Before our first exams, Naomi and I sat with our textbooks at the picnic tables beside the science block, watching a kid throw a piece of rockmelon to a magpie. An apple sticker was stuck under the clear contact of my library-issued chemistry textbook. I wondered: which librarian, which apple? Naomi got pissed off when I asked for her notes, but she handed them across the table anyway and I leaned over to kiss her cheek.

Mrs Cline ran the school ski trip and we all wanted to go. I'd landed a part-time job at the burger shop, high as a kite on the white and blue morning of my first shift, then going home to the dog licking chicken fat from my shoes. But Naomi didn't have a job, so after a couple of months I gave her a hundred dollars from the tissue box in my wardrobe, and she somehow saved the rest. I wanted Mrs Cline to like me, to know all the clever things going on in my brain, how I was going to change the world when I got my act together.

We did our chemistry exams in the school gym, spread out in desks alphabetically, and I chewed the gum that I'd hidden in my sock. Naomi's last name started with V so I knew I'd never be able to cheat off her. But Mrs Cline always told me I was a natural – does that explain how I got an A and Naomi got a B? After the exams came the parties. Naomi didn't get invitations to parties like I did, even though I told her over and over that she didn't need one. Nobody stood at the front door checking. At one party, after midnight, my boyfriend, Michael, went searching for his friend Joel, who'd left the party drunk. I took off after him, carrying my sandals because I liked how it looked to carry my sandals. We searched in all the front yards along Dominion Road; we stood on the bitumen in the snare of the streetlights when there were breaks in traffic. Finally, we found Joel in the lit-up neighbourhood park with a girl from my chemistry class. I knew she liked him, but the optics were off. I watched them sitting on the ground, on the bark chips, watching us, their backs against the wall of a plastic fort.

'Hi, Michael,' Joel said. 'Hi, Phoebe.'

I stared at my boyfriend's friend, feeling my desire but not saying a word.

In April, Michael and I broke up. There were falling leaves from liquid ambers along Trammer Creek while I cycled to school, always waiting for Joel to jog up and find me. On the school ski trip, stars scraped the sky above our cabin in the snow. Joel and I snuck out, unlatched the door to the games room and had sex – the scratchy, mossy couch, our icy fingertips. Rushes of snow against the glass like someone was above us, pouring water from a kettle. Michael didn't talk to me. Never spoke to me again.

One afternoon, Naomi, Rachel, Clare and I went to the town pool. We gossiped in the change rooms while we were in the middle of undressing because we liked how it looked: our grey skirts with bikini tops. Our school bags were open on the wet wooden benches and when our swim was over my chemistry textbook was gone. We found out that someone was caught spying with binoculars from the rooftop of the car dealership across the street. Naomi said, 'But come to the pool in person and you can see it in the flesh for free.' I had a feeling, always, of being watched.

I was ravenous, never sick, never got huge. I ate every bit of food in our kitchen. I stood over the stove dissolving chicken soup sachets into a salty, thin broth. I quit my part-time job and stayed at home, eating and studying. My chemistry textbook was never found, but the school got me a new one for free. Finally, I had to do my own homework. I graduated before Mum needed to buy me a bigger skirt.

A person's memory isn't a filing cabinet; it's pieces of modelling clay left on a shelf, waiting to be reshaped. The baby was something all the teachers would have known about. Me shaking my head at the guidance officer, trying to stop it all coming out. Me saying, *Please don't tell anyone.* Then early the next year, me having the baby – a boy. I've always stopped myself from describing what I felt when I saw him, and what I felt when I gave him away. They told me about the opportunity to seek contact eighteen years later, or not at all, ever again. The promise – I was able to sign what was needed – that I would defer to this future spectre, this young man's yes or his no.

Afterwards, Clare's dad gave me a job in town at his dermatology clinic, and I sat behind a desk, answering phones, a bit stunned. People were nice. Naomi dropped off an envelope filled with cash because she didn't know what else to do, and I cried with her there beside me. She stood in the doorway and barred a patient from coming in, told them the clinic was closing early.

~

On an aeroplane in 2009 in a cramped seat, the Texas panhandle below. Mrs Cline had understood what I was trying to do. I would leave Australia. I would study chemistry in the United States. I'd be reborn smarter, more hardworking. I'd find a bit of the world that needed changing.

Oil spill, off the coast of Florida, spring and summer 2010. Once-white birds were astonished-sticky. I went down to the coastline with a friend from college. We were high on the anticipation of doing a good deed, to be seen doing a good deed. We pulled in to buy gloves from a hardware store about an hour away but they were all sold out.

As a grad student in Virginia, I signed up to be a counsellor for a group of twelve-year-old girls on a camp sponsored by my university and a multinational company that had once dug for uranium in the Congo. I got a week away from my near-empty fridge and the hotbox that was my sharehouse. In the cafeteria of a fancy all-girls' college on my campus – one I'd never been to – I could tell which of the other counsellors were also there for the food. We avoided each other. At mealtimes I lined up with my tray and took warm white pots of baked veggies. I let the cheery workers drop great spoonfuls of mac and cheese onto my plate. At the salad bar I made painstaking salads garnished with nuts and chickpeas, and got my first meal of red meat in three months. The girls were nice. They expressed vague interests in physics, aeronautics, engineering, mining. They performed in team challenges, egging me on too – *Help us, Phoebe!* – like building a bridge out of newspapers. We all caught a bus and went roller skating. One of the girls in my group was deaf but could lip-read, and she gazed at me so intently every time I spoke that I felt a kinship, felt watched all over again. On the second-last night, after hot dogs and chocolate pudding, I even wondered if I could be a science teacher, flicking on Bunsen burners and pointing to a plastic skeleton while grateful, sunny children called out which bone was connected to which. But at the end of the week, I got my cheque for two hundred dollars and bought groceries and a new rice cooker, and soon forgot about those girls.

On my way to a conference to deliver the keynote, I stopped for petrol near Ottawa, Illinois, and on the TV was a man saying Deepwater Horizon wasn't nearly as bad as everyone liked to think. The oil hadn't even reached the shore, he said. Over the years, people's memories had deceived them. Anyone would have thought the whole state of Florida had been covered in oil! Very carefully, I replaced the nozzle in the bowser and covered my face so I wouldn't scream.

My head of faculty requested a meeting. He told me that after years of generous support, the university wouldn't be paying for research like mine anymore. The university had to change tack. It had to shore up in other ways. I could continue to expect contracts and teaching work, but in regard to financial support for the unusual direction my research was taking, I must seek other sources.

In Norway, in Stavanger, I made my way to the oil museum that hovered over the water in three buildings shaped like ocean rigs. Inside, hard flanks of polished stainless steel and mini bridges clanged with the sound of kids' boots. A brief history of petroleum was told in five feet of timeline against one wall. Buttons were for pressing, and tiny red lights lit up across a map of the North Sea. A school group in matching vests gathered around a simulator to learn the daily routines of an offshore worker. They lined up to enter something called a Catastrophe Room. At first I liked how danger was celebrated, and then I didn't. I thought of my baby and let my brain rest with those thoughts for a few seconds before shutting them away like the doors of a little cabinet. A few seconds were all I ever allowed myself. The boys in the crowd were fifteen, sixteen, seventeen. Eighteen.

In Bergen, I paid for a ticket on the funicular. There were only two of us on it. The man – Norwegian – talked to me in English about the mountain, the ride, the altitude, then he spoke about his wife and it seemed like he couldn't stop. She had left him, and then he had burnt many – but not all – of her things in a fit of anger, he could see that now. It was rage, not love. And now he was alone. He knew it was wrong to unload all this on a stranger, sorry, he was very sorry. We passed green pines, and the air was so clean it felt spicy in my nose. I thought that I would say a lot, knowing what I knew about loss, but I ended up saying nothing. The image of him tilting, his body humming on the edge of this mountain, the gondola motoring upwards then down. Him crying softly. Me, trying to picture this wife of his, wondering if she even existed.

Back out in the icy air, I hurried to a cafe a few blocks away, hoping it was the right one. I recognised *fish soup* on the menu. I recognised *rhubarb* and the word for *bread*. I placed my order and glanced up and there was Erik, the almost-retired researcher at UiB I'd been emailing. He picked his way over to me, manoeuvring his lanky body between tables. Tall and grinning and with a plume of soft grey hair that rose like steam from the crown of his head, he promised to show me the creatures.

Erik signed me in to his university lab then handed me goggles and gloves. We nodded to his colleagues. We would all go for beers later, Erik promised. Then he gestured towards a corner of the lab. He stood at my elbow. He called them *Kathari*, from the Greek, because they were his little cleaners. Under the microscope the bacteria were giddy, writhing rods. I knew this feeling of excitement. I felt it inside, moving outwards, radial. Long ago I'd realised that Mrs Cline had shepherded me through chemistry class. Of course she'd known about Naomi's homework notes, just as she'd known about the baby. But she must have seen something in me.

'Still a long way to go,' Erik said.

'I've got time,' I said.

Gently, he told me that whatever these creatures were offering us, perhaps we would be wrong to let them do it. We will feed them and feed them, happily absolving ourselves. If we can direct bacteria or insects to eat through our plastic, to gorge themselves on our spilt oil, then of course we will do it. All our energies will go to this, and not to other things. And when they can't eat the filth anymore, guess whose fault it will be?

'I know all this,' I said, smiling, trying to be charming. *Share your homework with me, please?*

'But at least it's a start,' he said.

'Erik,' I continued, 'humans are incapable of changing. But when we go out for beers, I'm still going to ask for your help.'

Alone again, I walked down to the fish markets on the harbour. Troll figurines were for sale alongside mounds of bristly crabs. Plush, silvery pelts were laid out on the cold stones. I didn't even know which animals had pelts like those. The day was starting to warm, the light in the sky rinsed and blue. The clouds ribbed across it in threads. I set myself up with a cup of coffee at a table outside a cafe and I rang the friend from college, the one I drove to Florida with all those years ago. She'd become a journalist, and I tried to read everything she wrote.

My hands were shaking. I asked her, 'How do I write what I need to write? How do I put such a thing into words, into something as thin and light as a letter? What will make him want to read on?'

'I don't know,' she said. 'I'm sorry. I'm thinking.'

'Assuming he even gets past the envelope, which he might toss straight in the bin. You're the writer,' I begged. 'Tell me.'

'Has it really been eighteen years?' she said. 'Shit.'

'I have this window, you see, and what if I scare him off?'

'Just be gentle,' she said. 'Tell him what you do with your time, what you've been doing.' In the background, I heard my friend's puppy barking, escalating in pitch and urgency.

'He's had his life,' I said. 'He might not even know I exist.'

~

I found myself on a beach near Mount Drummond, looking out at the inky water and fleecy waves of the Great Australian Bight. Rubber boots, wet weather gear, my long grey hair tucked under a woollen cap. My team couldn't see the drilling platform from where we sat. It was hundreds of kilometres out to sea. Years before, we'd protested the Norwegian oil company wanting to build its rigs, but of course they had won. They owned two wells out there. That beautiful, benign, life-giving word: *well*. But soon the spill – although they didn't call it that – would reach land.

On the sprawling, untidy beach, we bowed our heads together, our boots touching in the centre of the circle. I took a photo of our feet on the sand. I sent it to my son.

Because I didn't know precisely about the sort of life my son had had as a child, I was released, just a little, from the pain of thinking that the sort of childhood I had enjoyed – throwing stones into Trammer Creek and cannonballing into the town pool – might never exist again. It was clear to all of us on that beach that humanity stood on a precipice.

We unclasped our hands and stepped back. Getting the first letter from my son had felt as hopeful as this. For years he and I had been kind and careful with each other, nothing perfect. But we had muddled through. Maybe it's the best any of us can hope for.

My team and I set off in boats. Later, we released our *Kathari*, those hungry creatures, into the ocean.

AUTHOR NOTES

You Run Towards Love

1903 | MARIE CURIE | PHYSICS

One hundred years after Marie Curie became the first woman to win a Nobel Prize, Paris (like much of Europe in the summer of 2003) sweltered through a record-breaking heatwave. At this time, the French Government relaxed environmental laws to allow cooling water from nuclear reactors to be released into waterways at a higher temperature than normal. Marie was co-awarded the Nobel for her extraordinary research into radiation, after her husband, Pierre, insisted her name be included on the prize. In 1906 Pierre stepped onto a street in Paris and was struck and killed by a horse and cart, leaving behind Marie and their two daughters.

Grand Canyon

1911 | MARIE CURIE | CHEMISTRY

In 1921 American journalist Mrs William B. Meloney found out that Marie Curie had made no money from her discoveries. Curie's one wish was a single gram of radium, priced at $100,000, on which she would be able to conduct more experiments.

After failing to secure ten wealthy American women to give $10,000 each, Mrs Meloney crowdfunded the full amount from women all over the country. She coaxed Curie and her two daughters out from France and took them on a tour of the United States. President Harding gave Curie a golden key to a strongbox containing her gram of radium from the National Bureau of Standards, which she took home to Paris.

Something Close to Gold

1935 | IRÈNE JOLIOT–CURIE | CHEMISTRY

Fourteen years after this trip to the US, Irène Joliot-Curie, Marie's daughter, won for Chemistry, one of the few pairs of Nobel laureates who are related, and the only mother–daughter pair in history. French-born Joliot-Curie shared the prize with Frédéric Joliot, who was first her student, then her husband. Together, they experimented on polonium, boron, aluminium and magnesium. Their work resembled alchemy – transforming one element into another.

Night Blindness

1947 | GERTY THERESA CORI | PHYSIOLOGY OR MEDICINE

Gerty Cori's interest in science began when her father, who ran a sugar refinery in Prague, developed diabetes. Cori and her husband, Carl, worked together for years on various projects (Carl refused research roles if his wife was not given one too), including studies into metabolism and the effect of glucose on the body. Gerty was Jewish, Carl was Catholic, and the Coris migrated to New York in 1922 after Europe became a hostile place for Jewish people. A ferociously hard worker and a heavy smoker, Gerty developed xerophthalmia, likely from a vitamin A deficiency, while working at a hospital in prewar Vienna.

266

Hyperobject

1963 | MARIA GOEPPERT MAYER | PHYSICS

Philosopher Timothy Morton's concept of the 'hyperobject' encompasses the vastness, interconnectedness and reach of enormous objects, such as climate change and radioactive plutonium. Denise Kiernan's book *The Girls of Atomic City* provided insight into young women workers during World War II. Maria Mayer worked on the Manhattan Project to develop atomic bombs that were dropped on Japan in August 1945, bringing about the end of World War II. Born in Germany in 1906, but living out her final years in California, Mayer proposed the groundbreaking nuclear shell theory, which elucidated how electrons spin while they orbit a nucleus. She became only the second woman to receive the Physics Prize.

Frost

1964 | DOROTHY CROWFOOT HODGKIN | CHEMISTRY

Dorothy Hodgkin's win in 1964 signalled the first time women were awarded science Nobel Prizes in successive years. Born in Egypt and educated mostly in England, Hodgkin used x-ray crystallography to determine 3D biomolecular structures. She spent, for instance, thirty-five years deciphering the structure of insulin, a task that now takes scientists and modern computers mere hours or days. While researching at Somerville College, Oxford, Hodgkin tutored Margaret Roberts, later Prime Minister Thatcher. In 1953, Hodgkin was one of the first people to see Francis Crick and James Watson's model of the newly discovered double helix. In 1985, Hodgkin sat for a portrait by British artist Maggi Hambling, who painted the professor, in oils, working at her desk.

Stockholm

1977 | ROSALYN YALOW | PHYSIOLOGY OR MEDICINE

Rosalyn Yalow conducted revolutionary work with her long-time lab partner, Solomon 'Sol' Berson, that resulted in the radioimmunoassay – which provided the capacity to test for incredibly small measures of substances in liquids like water and blood. On 10 December 1977, Yalow collected her Nobel Prize without Berson, who died in 1972 (Nobels cannot be awarded posthumously). Yalow and Berson never patented their work, which had direct and far-reaching impacts on diabetes treatments and physicians' understanding of insulin, hepatitis and cancer. Yalow raised two children alongside her demanding lab schedule.

Corn Queen

1983 | BARBARA McCLINTOCK | PHYSIOLOGY OR MEDICINE

Barbara McClintock was a cytogeneticist and an ethnobotanist who became the first woman to win a Physiology or Medicine Nobel unshared with anyone else. McClintock hypothesised that chromosomes are protected by telomeres – a theory that would be taken up and tested by two later Nobel laureates. McClintock produced the first genetic map of corn, and spent most of her working life examining the cell behaviour of the plant. She pioneered research into transposition, studying how genes are regulated to alter physical characteristics. For years, McClintock recorded feeling alienated from other scientists because of her controversial ideas.

Growth

1986 | RITA LEVI-MONTALCINI | PHYSIOLOGY OR MEDICINE

Like Gerty Theresa Cori before her and Gertrude B. Elion after her, Rita Levi-Montalcini was inspired to work in the sciences after a loved one fell ill. Originally wanting to be an author, Levi-Montalcini changed her mind when her governess died of cancer, and she pursued medicine and neurobiology. She was banned, as many Jewish people were, from continuing to work in her university position in Mussolini's Italy. Instead, Levi-Montalcini set up a lab in her bedroom and experimented on fertilised chicken eggs she got from her neighbours. With Stanley Cohen, she co-discovered nerve growth factor.

Witnessing

1988 | GERTRUDE B. ELION | PHYSIOLOGY OR MEDICINE

In 1933, when Gertrude Elion was fifteen, her grandfather died of stomach cancer, inspiring her to pursue science. A biochemist and pharmacologist, Elion was unable, for a time, to obtain research positions commensurate with her skills. Later, she worked on drugs for leukaemia, herpes, cancer, malaria, HIV/AIDS and organ transplant recipients. Elion's drugs have saved millions of people, and for years she received letters of thanks from families whose lives were changed because of her research.

Fruit Flies

1995 | CHRISTIANE NÜSSLEIN-VOLHARD | PHYSIOLOGY OR MEDICINE

Christiane Nüsslein-Volhard grew up in post-World War II Germany. Curious about plants and animals, she decided at a young age that she wanted to be a biologist. Genes regulate the process by which embryonic cells divide and become specialised cells. Nüsslein-Volhard shared the prize in 1995 with Edward B. Lewis and Eric F. Wieschaus for their 'discoveries concerning the genetic control of early embryonic development'.

Nüsslein-Volhard told the Nobel Prize organisation that she was fascinated by flies, loved working with them, and that they followed her around in her dreams.

Titan Arum

2004 | LINDA B. BUCK | PHYSIOLOGY OR MEDICINE

American-born Linda Buck and her long-time collaborator, Richard Axel, determined how odorants are detected in the nose. In 1991 they published their revolutionary paper on odorant receptors. These receptors are located in a tiny part of the nasal cavity and, from there, messages are sent to parts of the brain. The differences in these signals allow human beings to distinguish, for example, between the scent of an apple and the scent of a strawberry, all of which was for a very long time unknown.

The Bodies Are Buried

2008 | FRANÇOISE BARRÉ-SINOUSSI | PHYSIOLOGY OR MEDICINE

French virologist Françoise Barré-Sinoussi was one of the first to discover what later became known as human immunodeficiency virus (HIV), which she identified in the context of understanding that it causes AIDS. Barré-Sinoussi and her chief collaborator, Luc Montagnier, made their discovery while working at the not-for-profit Pasteur Institute in Paris in the early 1980s. Barré-Sinoussi became president of the International AIDS Society, where she advocated for accessible antiretroviral drugs to improve the health of people living with HIV.

Better Nature

2009 | ADA E. YONATH | CHEMISTRY

Ada Yonath had an impoverished upbringing in Jerusalem. Later, as a keen young scientist, she took a job cleaning a laboratory and used the time alone to conduct her own experiments. When she was a crystallographer and professor at the Weizmann Institute of Science, Yonath won a Nobel for work she had started four decades earlier. She helped map the structure of ribosomes, using x-ray crystallography, which has had significant effects on the production of high-quality antibiotics. The last time a woman was awarded for Chemistry was forty-five years earlier when Dorothy Crowfoot Hodgkin's work – also in crystallography – was recognised.

Wingspan

2009 | ELIZABETH H. BLACKBURN | PHYSIOLOGY OR MEDICINE

Born in Hobart in 1948 into a family of two doctors and seven children, Elizabeth Blackburn was fascinated with the outdoor world. She was educated in Launceston and Melbourne, and is the only Australian woman to win a Nobel Prize in any field. Blackburn shared her 2009 win with Jack W. Szostak and her former student Carol W. Greider – the first time two women have shared the same prize. Blackburn, Szostak and Greider discovered telomerase, the enzyme that extends telomeres.

The Garden Bridge

2009 | CAROL W. GREIDER | PHYSIOLOGY OR MEDICINE

American-born Carol Greider shared the Nobel Prize in 2009 for her co-discovery, in 1984, of telomerase, which produces the DNA of telomeres. In their co-authored landmark paper published in *Cell* in 1985, Greider and her team refer to Nobel laureate Barbara McClintock's work on maize chromosomes. Their research is often cited as contributing to our understanding of the factors that affect our quality of life as we age. Telomeres deteriorate in all of us as we age but the rate differs. It appears possible to delay, prevent and even partially reverse their deterioration.

The Town Turns Over

2014 | MAY–BRITT MOSER | PHYSIOLOGY OR MEDICINE

Another husband-and-wife team, May-Britt and Edvard I. Moser won for 'their discoveries of cells that constitute a positioning system in the brain'. The positioning system they identified makes it 'possible to orient oneself in space, demonstrating a cellular basis for higher cognitive function'. Early in their careers, the Mosers studied psychology at the University of Oslo. Their research helps explain how human beings know which direction to go, and how to make repeat trips, all from memory. The parts of the brain that permit this navigation break down in people living with conditions such as Alzheimer's disease.

Little Fly

2015 | TU YOUYOU | PHYSIOLOGY OR MEDICINE

Malaria kills hundreds of thousands of people per year and, according to the World Health Organization, children under five make up around sixty per cent of all deaths. Working from her laboratory at the China Academy of Traditional Chinese Medicine in Beijing, Tu Youyou consulted Chinese texts dating back 1600 years and isolated an anti-malarial compound from a plant that had traditionally been used to treat malaria. *Qinghaosu*, or artemisinin, has led to improved health outcomes for millions of patients affected by malaria. In her lab, Tu demonstrated her confidence in its safety and efficacy: she first tested it on herself.

The Fix

2018 | DONNA STRICKLAND | PHYSICS

Canadian optical physicist Donna Strickland and her PhD supervisor, Gérard Mourou, invented chirped pulse amplification by stretching, amplifying then recompressing laser pulses. Doctors use these high-intensity, extremely brief pulses of light beams to perform precise cuts during, for example, laser eye surgery. Strickland is the third woman, after Curie and Mayer, to win the Physics Prize, and only the second Canadian woman laureate in any field. Strickland's Nobel win was awarded on the basis of her first scientific paper, published with Mourou in 1985.

A Brief History of Petroleum

2018 | FRANCES H. ARNOLD | CHEMISTRY

Frances Arnold is a chemical engineer, inventor and entrepreneur working out of the California Institute of Technology. She pioneered directed evolution to change the function of enzymes, whereby enzymes can conduct new or faster or better chemical reactions. Directed evolution employs what nature has been doing for millennia: selecting genetic mutations within an organism that impart advantageous properties. Specific applications of Arnold's research include more-sustainable pharmaceutical substances and renewable fuels, often with fewer by-products.

ACKNOWLEDGEMENTS

THANK YOU TO MY WONDERFUL PUBLISHER, Aviva Tuffield, who has been an encouraging presence in my writing life for many years. Aviva understood this project in its early days and worked so hard to help me shape it. Cathy Vallance is a careful, genius editor – thank you. I'm really grateful to the whole team at UQP.

I wrote this book with generous support from the Australia Council for the Arts, Varuna the Writers' House, *Griffith Review*, and a Queensland Writers Fellowship through State Library of Queensland and Arts Queensland. Versions of the following stories were first published online and in print: 'Something Close to Gold' in *New Australian Fiction*, 2019; 'Fruit Flies' in *Overland*, issue 236, 2019; 'Wingspan' in *Griffith Review*, edition 58, 2017; 'The Garden Bridge' in *Overland*, issue 235, 2019; 'The Town Turns Over' in *Griffith Review*, edition 68, 2020. Thank you to the editors of these publications.

I'm grateful to Ashley Hay, who was a wise and insightful mentor when my ideas were fledgling. Thanks to Rebecca Pouwer for answering lots of my questions. Thank you, yet again, to the wonderful Ian See. Thank you, John Tague. My gratitude to the following people for their assistance with various details, drafts, or crises of confidence: Tamara Armstrong, Brooke Davis, Jonathan Hadwen, Sarah Kanake, Andrew Last and Jack Vening. For their time and expertise, I thank Åsa Husberg and Karin Jonsson of the Nobel Prize Museum, Stockholm.

Thanks to the stars in my writing groups: Andrea Baldwin, Sean Di Lizio, Emma Doolan, Kathy George and Kate Zahnleiter, all of whom are so generous with their time and ideas. And I could not have finished this book without Mirandi Riwoe's support and friendship.

Thanks to my in-laws for their enthusiasm and help, and my great friends who cheer me on. Love and gratitude to my supportive, beautiful parents and infinitely good sister, Jiselle. And final thanks and love to Simon, Harriet and Theo. Our lives are full and busy and it's hard to get away to write. But all I want to do when I'm away is come back home to you.